"I'm here to stay."

"It's too dangerous for you," Jake said, fatigue and defeat in his tone. "I'm sorry, but I have to keep you safe."

"I understand you're a worried father and you're hurting because you feel so helpless. But you got me involved, and I'm the only one who can draw this killer out. Let me do that, Jake."

He fisted his hands, his hard-edged expression reminding her of a wall of rock. Hard to reach, hard to handle, but so easy to love.

"Jake..."

He looked at her, and she saw it all in his eyes. The need, the fear, the regret and the longing.

He let out a deep breath. "I've got to find her, Ella. I can't rest till I do."

"Yes, you can," she replied. "You'll rest while I take over for you."

"And when will you rest?"

"After we find your daughter...and get this madman. Or I die trying."

He touched her cheek. "And that's what scares me the most."

Books by Lenora Worth

Love Inspired Suspense

A Face in the Shadows
Heart of the Night
Code of Honor
Risky Reunion
Assignment: Bodyguard
The Soldier's Mission
Body of Evidence
The Diamond Secret
Lone Star Protector
In Pursuit of a Princess
Forced Alliance
Deadly Holiday Reunion

Love Inspired

When Love Came to Town◊
Something Beautiful◊
Lacey's Retreat◊
Easter Blessings
  "The Lily Field"
†*The Carpenter's Wife*
†*Heart of Stone*
†*A Tender Touch*
  Blessed Bouquets
  "The Dream Man"

*A Certain Hope
*A Perfect Love
*A Leap of Faith
  Christmas Homecoming
  Mountain Sanctuary
  Lone Star Secret
  Gift of Wonder
  The Perfect Gift
  Hometown Princess
  Hometown Sweetheart
  The Doctor's Family
  Sweetheart Reunion
  Sweetheart Bride
  Bayou Sweetheart

Steeple Hill

  After the Storm
  Echoes of Danger
  Once Upon a Christmas
    "'Twas the Week Before Christmas"

◊In the Garden
†Sunset Island
*Texas Hearts

LENORA WORTH

has written more than forty books for three different publishers. Her career with Love Inspired Books spans close to fifteen years. In February 2011, her Love Inspired Suspense novel *Body of Evidence* made the *New York Times* bestseller list. Her very first Love Inspired title, *The Wedding Quilt,* won *Affaire de Coeur*'s Best Inspirational for 1997, and *Logan's Child* won an *RT Book Reviews* Best Love Inspired for 1998. With millions of books in print, Lenora continues to write for the Love Inspired and Love Inspired Suspense lines. Lenora also wrote a weekly opinion column for the local paper and worked freelance for years with a local magazine. She has now turned to full-time fiction writing and enjoying adventures with her retired husband, Don. Married for thirty-six years, they have two grown children. Lenora enjoys writing, reading and *shopping*...especially shoe shopping.

DEADLY
HOLIDAY REUNION

LENORA WORTH

HARLEQUIN® LOVE INSPIRED® SUSPENSE

Recycling programs for this product may not exist in your area.

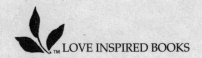

™ LOVE INSPIRED BOOKS

ISBN-13: 978-0-373-44630-8

Deadly Holiday Reunion

www.Harlequin.com

Printed in U.S.A.

God is my strength and power:
and he maketh my way perfect.
—*2 Samuel* 22:33

For all of my East Texas friends.
You are all Texas Strong!

ONE

"I need you to help me find my daughter."

Ella Terrell hushed her barking German shepherd and stared up at the tall man standing with his cowboy hat in his hand at the door of the barn.

Jake Cavanaugh.

"What?" Her pulse quickened, causing her to put down the rifle she had aimed at him and squint into the sun. Even though he lived and worked a few miles away in Tyler, Texas, she hadn't seen him or heard a word from him in over five years. Pushing away the dark memories surfacing in her mind, she asked, "What are you doing here, Jake? What do you mean?"

He shifted, turned to glance around the tree-lined yard toward the house, the star emblem on his Texas Ranger badge flashing gold. "Look, I don't have much time and I haven't slept all night." Then he lowered his head but lifted his gaze to her. "Ella, I need your help. Somebody took Macey."

The plea in his golden-brown eyes did her in. Jake had never been good at asking for help. Which only showed how desperate he must be to come to her. Ella had left the FBI a few years before, but if Macey was missing, she'd help Jake find her.

Ella nodded and took him by the elbow to guide him

up to the house, her big dog trailing behind them. "Let's get inside and talk."

When they reached the house, Ella hurried up the porch and waited as Jake pushed his way past the big evergreen Christmas wreath hanging on the door, his broad shadow temporarily blocking out the warmth of the Texas sun.

Once inside, he pivoted back to stare at Ella, his expression dark with worry. "Macey was kidnapped last night."

Macey, the daughter he'd had with another woman after he'd broken off his engagement to Ella. Having a child at nineteen hadn't been easy. Having a wife who got sick with cancer eight years later had been the worst. Jake's wife, Natalie, had died and left him with a little girl to raise.

Ella rubbed a grubby hand over her ponytail then snapped into action. Putting down the rifle she always kept with her when she was working alone, she motioned toward the kitchen. "C'mon in and tell me everything."

Giving her a thankful nod, Jake stepped into the old farmhouse and did a quick sweep of the staircase and den.

Sensing his agitation, Ella motioned to the long dining table between the den and kitchen. "My grandparents went into town for supplies." She pointed to the big dog that had followed them inside. "Just me and Zip. I have fresh coffee."

Jake plopped down on a chair and laid his hat on the table near a glazed pot holding a bright red poinsettia. He looked exhausted. His eyes, always a bright golden-brown that reminded her of a cougar, looked washed out and dull. He looked a lot older than his thirty-four years. She couldn't help but compare this Jake to the one who'd angrily told her close to sixteen years ago that they couldn't get married if she was going to become an FBI agent like her daddy. She remembered every word of their conversation.

"But, Jake, we've talked about this. It'll be years before

I can prepare to take the applicant test. We'll get married after we graduate college, just like we planned. Once we're done with school, we can both work toward our careers."

"And what about a house full of children, Ella? We've talked about that, too. I know you want to follow in your daddy's footsteps, but I thought you'd get over that notion once we got married. It's too dangerous and it'll be hard on a family."

"And I've supported your choice to become a Texas Ranger, but I guess I was the only one being honest about things. I want children but I also want to work for the FBI. You've always known that. Why are you worried about children now? If you get to be a Ranger, why can't I do what I want? We can still have children."

He'd refused to listen, had accused her of not really loving him. Ella figured underneath the bluster of his complaints, he'd really been trying to protect her and maybe keep her from doing something out of a sense of duty, but they'd been young and stupid and stubborn, and neither of them had backed down. So they'd broken up during the summer they'd planned to be married.

Maybe now they'd both aged and become a little wiser, but she could still see the stubbornness in the set of his jaw and the gleam of his eyes. It was the same stubbornness she'd seen when they'd teamed up again five years ago to track a killer. After that ordeal had ended…they'd gotten close again.

But Ella didn't want to think about all the reasons she'd had to say no to Jake a second time. Maybe she wasn't the marrying kind, after all.

Ella brought him his coffee and sat down with her own cup, memories of his sweet little daughter churning in her soul. Of course, Macey would be a teenager now. Her hand rubbing Zip's soft fur, she asked, "What happened, Jake?"

"She…uh…" He took a breath, pinched two fingers

over his nose. "Somebody took her. Out of her friend's car. Last night at the mall."

Ella nodded, trying to encourage him to go on. Jake wasn't one to show emotions so he had to stop and clear his throat several times.

"Have you heard anything? Seen anything?" And because she couldn't stop thinking it, she added, "And why do you need me, Jake? You're a Texas Ranger. You've tracked criminals all over this state. All over the country."

She knew firsthand how good he was at his job. He'd found her once when she was near death. She wouldn't think of that, or of how she'd broken his heart again after he'd found her. What it must have cost him to come here for her help.

Jake held his coffee mug with both hands, his head down. "This is different. This is Macey." He gave her a glance that told Ella he wanted to say more.

"Why'd you come to *me?*" she asked again, her mind already clicking back into a professional mode. "You know I left the FBI, right?"

Jake grabbed her hand, his eyes centered on her face. "Ella, listen to me. *He* took her. That's why I'm here."

Ella's heart rate surged like a storm coming over the pasture and then crashed into a thundering warning. "Do you know the man who took Macey?"

Jake's eyes filled with a bright anger and then he nodded. "We both know him. The Dead Drop Killer. He took my little girl. And I need you to help me find her before it's too late."

Ella clutched her hands to the lip of the old oak table. "The Dead Drop Killer? No." She got up and paced around the big country kitchen, her gaze hitting on her grandmother's cross-stitching. The lacy white dish towels with the bright red-and-green holly leaves etched on their edges looked perfectly ordinary. "No, no, Jake. He's…he's gone. He hasn't killed anyone in over five years because he's dead. The trail ran cold after you found me. You know that. You know he was wounded and…he had to have died in those woods, possibly drowned in the lake. You were there the night—"

"I was there the night I found you half-dead and just about out of your mind," Jake said. "Yeah, I remember everything about that night and everything that happened afterward. But we never found a body, Ella." He shook his head. "We assumed he was dead but we never actually had proof."

His eyes held accusation as well as torment. He'd never forgiven her for following her dream, but he'd sure brought home the point he'd tried to make when they broke up way back. Being an FBI agent was dangerous.

And some dangers never went away.

Ella gulped in air, ran to the back window and stared out over the fence line leading down to Caddo Lake. A beautiful winter day waited for her but she could only see the dark, murky memories clouding out the sun. "It's been so long. So long. We thought he'd drowned. Out in the lake." She whirled around. "I'm comfortable here now. I found something I could do and I love it. Something to help me heal."

Jake got up and came to her. Putting his hands on her arms, he stared down at her. "He's back. And he took my Macey."

Ella refused to believe that. "How do you know it's him?"

Jake tugged a small brown evidence bag out of his shirt pocket. "Because of this—the first clue." He carefully opened the bag and turned it down just enough that she could see what was inside without touching it. "He left me a note that led me to this."

Ella gasped, her gaze slipping over the necklace. A delicate gold chain with a white daisy hanging from it. The chain Jake had given Ella for graduation their senior year of high school.

The chain she'd been wearing several years after high school and a lifetime later when the case they'd been working on together had gone bad and the Dead Drop Killer had taken Ella and held her here on Caddo Lake with the intent to kill her in the same way he'd killed four other young women. But she'd escaped because she had been trained to survive. Special Agent Ella Terrell. She'd lived, but they'd never caught the man who'd taken her. She'd wounded him during her escape and some had believed he'd crawled off like the animal he was and died in the woods. Some thought the alligators had done away with him. Others had predicted he'd come back one day. Some of the rumors said he still lived in the woods—waiting for her.

Ella had refused to believe those rumors. Just high school kids trying to scare each other. But the Dead Drop Killer preferred young, dark-haired girls. Girls like Macey Cavanaugh. Girls with hair similar to Ella's—back then. He'd taken Ella to make a point, to show her that he could break her, training or no training, because she'd gotten too close.

At least that was what she believed. Some of the old team members believed she'd been his target all along, but her mind couldn't comprehend that after four deaths. Why would he want her so badly?

But in the end, maybe he'd succeeded in breaking her. He hadn't killed her, but she certainly hadn't been able to do her job anymore. And now Jake was asking her to step back into that world....

She slammed a fist against her old jeans, logic slamming against fear inside her head.

They'd never found his body and they'd never found her

necklace. This was that same necklace. Of that she had no doubt. She could see the old, dried bloodstains caked against the links of gold. She hated daisies.

"No, no." She reached out, grabbed at Jake's plaid shirt. "No, Jake. He can't...it can't be him."

"I think it is, honey," Jake replied, the truth charging through his eyes. "I came to you because you're the only one who can help me find him—and because I'm worried about you. I've got a little bit of a head start before a task force from Tyler shows up with the Sheriff's Office."

He pushed at the bangs falling over Ella's forehead. "I'm sorry but I need you, Ella. I'm going to track him."

His touch was as gentle against her skin as a butterfly's fluttering wings. But the look in his eyes was anything but gentle. "And this time, when I do find him I'm going to kill him."

Jake watched as Ella went around, gathering supplies and firearms. She obviously knew how to take care of herself. She'd been doing it for years now. She had a loyal guard dog to warn her of strangers. Zip had alerted her that someone was approaching when Jake arrived and she'd greeted him there in the barn with a rifle pointed at his head. Nothing new about a Texan carrying a weapon on her own land, but Ella needed the security of protecting herself more than most after what she'd been through.

"You seemed prepared to hold off an army," he said to settle his antsy nerves. He glanced at the huge Christmas tree by the picture window, memories of other Christmases lighting his mind.

Now she turned to explain, one hand tugging through her burnished gold-streaked hair. Hair that used to be a rich brown. Had she dyed it? "I have weapons hidden inside the house and out in the barn. Even in the open-air dining room down by the lake." She lifted her chin in defiance, just the way she'd done when they'd fought long ago. "I won't live in a spirit of fear."

Jake had to agree with that. God's people *didn't* live in a spirit of fear, but it paid to be prepared, too. "But you live with your grandparents," he said. "They'll need to know what's going on."

She'd have to send them away. Somewhere safe.

She nodded, went back to gathering supplies. "They'll be home any minute now. I'll close down the restaurant for a while." Her sky-blue eyes went dark. "We'll set up the command post here."

Jake didn't want to rush her, but each minute was precious. He had to talk to keep from screaming. "Uh, so you run a restaurant now. I saw the sign on the gate. Caddo Country?"

Ella's gaze swept over the den and kitchen in an urgent rush. "Yes, it's farm-to-table meals by request out underneath the big screened gazebo and outdoor kitchen Grandpa helped me build." She checked her weapons, grabbed ammunition.

Jake let her do her thing, figuring Ella needed to feel safe and he'd see to it that she was safe. But he could tell she'd left the law enforcement life behind. She'd built more than a restaurant here. She'd rebuilt her life. Without Jake. Had she ever really needed him?

"I have to keep them away, Jake," she said now. "You know they raised me after my parents died." She stopped, stared off into space. "I can't believe he's back."

Jake could tell she was reliving the terrible memories and the awful guilt of knowing one man had killed four young women just possibly so he could get to Ella. One faceless man who now had his daughter.

"I don't know for sure if it's him, but the MO is the same."

"You need to brief me before we get going."

He cleared his throat and wished he didn't need to do

this. "A whole lot of law enforcement people are out there looking, but I knew once I found that necklace I had to come and check on you."

Ella whirled to stare at him. "And you also knew I'd want to help."

"Yeah. I didn't want you to hear this news from anybody else. I figured you'd strike out on your own to find him."

"And Macey," she added before she turned back to her busywork. "I'd have to find Macey."

He couldn't lie. "Yes. I really need you to help me figure out the clues and stay on this, Ella. We don't have much time."

Ella's sky-colored eyes met his with a look of defiance, chased by a solid trepidation. "No, we don't. But if this is him, then neither does he."

Jake went silent while they both remembered what this man could do to a victim. He could see that horror written all over Ella's face.

TWO

After Ella left the FBI, she came home to East Texas. At first, she only wanted to heal and get her bearings and maybe prove to herself that she still had courage to face those dense woods each day. But weeks had stretched into months and, finally, she'd resigned from her Dallas post and she'd never looked back.

Until now.

Jake followed her, checking weapons right behind her. Not used to him being around and certainly not nearly prepared for what he'd told her, she whirled around and gave him a nasty glare.

"Sorry," he said, his gaze holding hers. "Old habits—"

"I can't have you doing that, Jake," she told him. "I need to think this through. He—whoever took Macey—told you he'd leave the next…drop…somewhere near Caddo Lake? That's a lot of territory. So tell me everything about last night."

Jake stood her Remington against the old hutch, but seemed to hesitate. What was he not telling her?

"I can't help you if you don't tell me everything," she said with an air of gentle frustration. "I can take it."

He nodded, glanced over at the Remington. "Took her from a car at the mall in Tyler just after closing time. She'd gone shopping with a friend after work, for a party dress.

Her boyfriend, Luke Hurst, lives not far from here and he'd invited her to a Christmas dance." Jake stopped and Ella watched as he reined in his emotions with a tight-lipped determination. "She was all excited about that dance."

He went silent, then took in a breath. "The kidnapper apparently managed to park right next to them and when Macey went to get in on the passenger's side, he hopped out of the driver's side of his vehicle and used his open door to block her. So he grabbed her, held a gun to her head and shoved her into the truck, then got in and took off."

"And the friend?"

"Rachel. Her best friend. Screamed her head off as she watched the pickup driving away."

Ella's heart hammered at the terrifying memories grabbing at her consciousness. Sweaty, dirty hands on her mouth and body. A gun held to her head. A sense of helplessness that she sometimes felt creeping back like a spider crawling on her skin.

"Description?"

"A dark hood and dark glasses, maybe a beard. The other girl was already behind the wheel in her car and it happened so fast, she didn't get a good look at him. Said the truck was dark, maybe black. But she couldn't tell us the make or model."

"License plate?"

"Said she couldn't see one in the dark. She was pretty shook up when the police called me."

"And the boyfriend?"

"I've left messages, but his parents told me he works nights in town and sometimes doesn't answer his phone when he's at work. I came here first, but I've got people checking on him, too." He checked his pocket pad notes. "Rachel—the friend Macey was with—knows Luke, though. She swears it wasn't him and I believe her."

"And when did you get the first clue?"

"Around midnight last night." He sank back down on a chair. "I combed every inch of the mall and the surrounding neighborhoods. No black truck, no witnesses other than her friend. I went back to the mall to talk to the Tyler Police. When I got back to my truck, I saw a note on the dash. White paper, cutout letters of various sizes pasted on it."

Just like the Dead Drop Killer. He never used phones or computers. Only left a paper trail leading to clues he called dead drops. Clues that he hid in obscure, out-of-the-way places and that worked like a scavenger hunt. The next of kin and law enforcement agencies had to follow the clues in hopes of reaching the victims in time.

They never made it.

They'd found all of the girls dead. Four of them over a two-year period until about five years ago. Five years ago, Ella had almost become his fifth victim. A decoy to flush out a killer, only the killer had somehow figured things out. Because, according to the profilers, the killer had always only wanted Ella. No one could explain why he might be obsessed with her. The theories ranged from the killer being someone from her father's case files or maybe the killer hated FBI agents in general. They'd never traced him back to her because they'd been so intent on finding the last girl he killed.

Ella didn't think he wanted *her* to seek revenge. She just believed he was an evil, sick man who'd almost gotten caught and he'd taken her to possibly have another victim. He'd never explained himself when he'd held her. He'd barely talked to her except to tell her he would kill her if she didn't do as he asked. But he'd always called her "Sweet Ella."

Jake, by then a seasoned lawman, had been on the team trying to find her. He'd been the one *to* find her. That case had brought them back together for the first time since high school, but neither of them had been ready for a true relationship. Or a second chance.

He'd just lost his wife six months earlier and…after he'd rescued Ella, she'd been in no shape to make a commitment to anyone.

You survived, Ella kept telling herself. *You made it out alive.*

But things had been different in her case. The killer knew she was FBI, knew she wanted to find him and bring him to justice. He'd lured her out with a special set of dead drops put up just for Ella. As if he'd been waiting for her to come.

She'd found him but he'd almost killed her. And he'd broken her. If it hadn't been for her faith and her grandparents' strong, enduring love, Ella probably would have curled up and died.

Pushing away the tremors moving up her backbone, she asked, "So what did the note say?"

Jake paced in front of the decorated fireplace. "Told me to go alone to a pavilion on the west side of the lake and look on the picnic table closest to the boat launch. I found the necklace dangling off a nail."

She whirled around to stare at him. "And you must have found his next note."

Jake nodded, tugged at his clipped light brown hair. "White paper, nailed on a nearby tree. 'Tell Ella I miss her.'"

Ella hands trembled in spite of her clenched jaw. "He sent you to me."

Jake started for her but stopped. "I'm sorry, Ella. He knows I'd come here and I had to come. For Macey's sake. And to make sure you're okay."

"Do I look okay?"

"I'm sorry," he said again. "I should have killed him when I had a chance."

But he'd stayed with her instead. Because when he'd found her curled up in a ball against a cypress tree like a wounded, dying animal, Ella had latched on to him and begged him never to leave her again.

Delirious. She'd been dehydrated and delirious and… Jake had taken her into his arms and held her. While the killer got away. They'd searched almost every inch of the lake and the surrounding areas and they'd put out APBs and a BOLO, but they'd never found the wounded killer.

She put that out of her mind. Remembered how she'd pushed Jake away after he'd come to see her in the hospital. Remembered how she'd once loved him and wanted to marry him.

She'd been too damaged and broken and burned out after her ordeal to handle what she considered his disapproval. Too damaged to go back into a relationship with the man she'd loved since high school, a man who'd become a Texas Ranger. Jake loved his job but after her two short years as a federal agent Ella hated anything having to do with criminals and lawmen. She'd become a coward. A big, scared coward. Jake's wife had died the year before Ella's ordeal and he'd deserved so much more than Ella could give.

Now, five years later, he'd come to her again but she'd only just begun to heal.

Finally.

She was headed right back into the nightmare but she couldn't say no to Jake. Not when that madman might have his daughter.

Ella said a prayer for courage. "Okay, he's got our attention. What next?"

Jake gave her a look that told her everything but said nothing. "I think he's going back to the scene of his last crime."

Ella's head jerked at that. "You think he's got Macey somewhere on the lake?"

"I think he's brought her to the place where he brought you." He shifted on his boots. "He didn't get to finish that job."

The place where he'd brought her to die. The killer had dragged her all over East Texas and then back to the place he knew she loved. Caddo Lake.

She could still remember his hot breath on her neck, could still see the black mask he always wore and the intensity of the last few words he'd spoken to her. "You'll never be found, dear one. The alligators and snakes will take care of you. Here on your beloved Caddo Lake."

The authorities decided the alligators and other creatures had taken care of his body instead.

Ella held her eyes tightly shut. "I believed he'd died in the woods or had drowned." She shook her head. "I wanted to believe that. But I always wondered…."

"Ella…"

She wouldn't give in to the tremendous need to rush into Jake's arms. She had to keep it together for Macey's sake. It wasn't Macey's fault that her mother had taken Ella's high school sweetheart and made him hers by getting herself pregnant, only to up and die on him. And it wasn't Macey's fault that five years ago when another girl had turned up missing, circumstances had brought Jake and Ella back together to help track the killer and that girl. Nor was it Macey's fault that fate had pushed them together again today.

Sometimes Ella dreamed of being back in high school and instead of telling Jake she wanted to become an FBI agent, she wished she'd told him yes, she'd marry him and be his wife and live a simple life out in the country while he worked at becoming a Texas Ranger.

It wasn't anyone's fault that they would never be able

to get back to that place of love and need that had once colored their world in sweet shades of amber and gold.

But it was the Dead Drop Killer's fault that she was standing here with this Texas Ranger and her Remington, about to go back out into those woods that had held her captive for so long that she still had nightmares about them.

That was the killer's fault and because she had to help Jake find his daughter, Ella now had one more chance to do what she should have done all those years ago.

So she nodded at Jake and dropped extra ammo into her rucksack. "He's probably left something here at the farm. We need to get out there and find the next clue."

THREE

Ella opened the front door but Zip rushed past her, the big dog's light bark alerting Jake and Ella that someone had arrived at the Terrell farm.

"Who is it?" Jake asked as he automatically moved in front of Ella to shield her.

"My grandparents," she replied, purposely stepping around him. "If it had been a stranger, Zip would have barked loudly and knocked us over getting to them."

"Good dog," Jake said. He brushed a hand over the big dog's chocolate-brown top coat. At least he could rest easy that Ella had set measures in place to protect herself.

But this killer had been known to get around any type of security measures. As far as Jake could tell, Ella had only the dog and her few weapons scattered around to keep her safe. Far too vulnerable.

"What are you gonna tell them?" he asked, his anxiety at top level. He had to get out into those woods and find Macey before he went stark-raving mad. Once that task force showed up and the killer found out, Macey could be dead before nightfall. This man would savor the attention but he could be pushed too far, too fast if they weren't careful.

"The truth," Ella replied. She set down her rucksack

and her rifle. "I'll hurry. I know you're anxious to get on with it."

Jake nodded. It didn't take much to see that, but Ella had always known how to read his moods. Swallowing back the deep pit of fear that had clutched his gut since he'd gotten the call last night, Jake continued the silent, screaming prayer he'd been reciting since he'd realized just who might have his daughter.

Protect her, Lord. Protect my baby girl. And help me to do my job to the best of my ability. For all of our sakes.

Ella stepped forward to help her elderly grandparents with the groceries. Jake did the same.

Grandpa Terrell stared through his bifocals. "Edna, we got company for our noon meal."

Edna Terrell's smiling face greeted Jake as he reached to take a bag from her. "My, my, is this Jake Cavanaugh I'm seeing here with my own eyes?"

"It's me," Jake said, shooting a glance toward Ella. "How you doing?"

"We're just fine as frog hair," Edna replied with a laugh. "What in the world brings you all the way out here on this chilly day?"

Ella stared up at her granddaddy with solemn eyes. Wilson Terrell was a shrewd, smart man. He nodded at Jake as if he knew something was up. "Good to see you, Jake."

Ella held a sack of groceries and guided her grandmother up to the house. "We were about to leave," she began. "Jake needs my help on…a case."

She went on inside and waited for Jake and her grandpa.

Now even cheery Miss Edna had gathered something was wrong. She took off her glasses, her gaze darting between the two of them. "What kind of case, honey?"

Ella put a hand on her grandmother's arm. "Listen, Granny. I need you and Grandpa to take Zip and go into

Gilmer for a few days. You can stay with Aunt Rosalyn, okay?"

"Why?" Edna asked, her blue eyes moving from Ella to Jake. "What is it?"

Ella's look of fear cut Jake to the core. He didn't want to put her through this again but he had no choice. He had to save Macey. He'd lost so much in his life—first Ella after their breakup, then Natalie had died and a few years after that both his parents had gone on to heaven just two years apart. Macey was the only good thing he had left. And Ella was the only woman who could understand what he and his daughter were going through.

Ella tried to speak, then glanced over to him, a look of panic and doubt clouding her heart-shaped face.

"We have reason to believe the Dead Drop Killer is back on the loose, Miss Edna. He's taken another girl."

Edna put a hand to her heart. "Oh, no. I thought he was dead and gone." She grabbed Ella by the hands. "You can't go back out there, honey. You're not prepared for this. Let Jake take care of it."

Ella gave her grandmother a wistful glance. "I have to help, Granny. Jake needs me."

Wilson stepped forward to put his arm around his wife's shoulder then scowled at Jake. "Why would you come here and put her through this again? That man is dead. You don't need her for anything else."

Jake held up a hand then let it drop. This time Ella had to do the talking.

"He has Macey, Grandpa," Ella said, her voice cracking for the first time since he'd told her. "He has Jake's daughter. And he's already left clues in this area. We think he has her somewhere on the lake."

Edna sank down on a chair. "Mercy me, I can't believe this is happening again." She gave Jake a look full of understanding. "What can we do?"

"Do what Ella has asked," he said through the lump in his throat. "Go somewhere safe."

"We can defend ourselves," Wilson said, his backbone straightening. "Got guns and Zip. And I'm still a pretty good shot."

"You can't protect yourselves from this, Grandpa," Ella said. "Please do this for me. I can't help Jake if I'm worried about the two of you. Call Aunt Rosalyn and tell her…tell her you need to stay with her for a few days."

"But she'll wonder—"

"No one else can know what we're doing for now," Jake said, shaking his head. "No police except for the team in Tyler that's already involved. They're doing what they can but I'm off the grid for a while. Just me and Ella on this one for now."

"I don't like that idea," Wilson retorted. "You need to bring in the sheriff and get some more Rangers out here."

"The sheriff is aware of the situation and he's working behind the scenes. I don't like going it alone, either, sir. But that madman will kill my daughter if he thinks we've brought in a whole passel of law enforcement. We'll call for backup when the time comes."

"Or when it's too late, like last time," Wilson retorted. "But then I shouldn't have to remind either of you—"

"Grandpa, it's okay. We'll alert the kidnapper if we set up a command post anywhere near these woods. The Tyler Police Department and the FBI have a task force in place, right, Jake?"

Jake nodded. "Set it up late last night. They know where I am and they're working on every angle and waiting to hear, but right now, I need to get out there and see what I can find."

"I still don't like it," Wilson said. "You're using my granddaughter as a decoy again. It's too dangerous. Same as what happened last time."

Edna went to him and patted his shoulder. "Shhh. Jake's got enough to worry about without you bringing up things we can't change."

Jake lowered his head. Ella's granddaddy had a right to blame him for Ella's ordeal. He'd been the lead investigator since the killer had taken the last girl into his territory. But Ella had been called in to help because she'd worked two of the other cases and because she knew these woods. Who could have predicted that the killer knew these piney woods, too? The Dead Drop Killer had set a convincing trap for Ella by having the girl call her for help and because she wanted to save a life, she'd walked right into it.

They'd have to keep that in mind and be diligent this time, not only for Ella's sake but to keep Macey alive, too.

"I'll be smart," Ella said, her tone not so convincing, her big eyes wide. "I'll be with Jake."

"I won't leave her side," Jake said, hoping he sounded a little more confident than Ella. "This time, I'll make sure she stays safe. I promise."

At least Ella had given him a vote of confidence. He needed her to trust him and in this case, he needed her to lead him. He was too distraught to think straight. Ella would help him snap out of that so he could focus on finding Macey.

His little girl. She was a blossoming teenager now but she was still his baby. Images of lacy party dresses and dainty diamond earrings seared through his raw nerves, only to be followed by other images he had to get out of his head. He glanced at Edna Terrell and saw the compassion in her eyes.

It almost brought Jake to his knees. "Can you do me one more favor, Miss Edna?"

"Of course," the gray-haired lady replied.

"Pray," he said.

Edna nodded then stood up and hugged him close. "Of course we will."

It took a few more minutes of persuasion but finally, Ella called her aunt and explained that the farm was having safety problems. The restaurant would be shut down for the next few days and possibly longer.

Apparently, her aunt hadn't questioned her. When Ella hung up, she turned to her grandparents. "She's looking forward to having y'all over. I know we live only an hour or so away, but she misses y'all so go and rest and I'll check in as often as I can."

"You'd better," Edna said, her gaze on Jake. "I'll go pack a few things while Wilson puts away the groceries."

Ella explained to Jake that the restaurant was only open for reserved private dinners on request and closed on Mondays, so she called the handful of employees who worked at Caddo Country and explained that she'd decided since they didn't have any bookings till later this month, she was shutting down the kitchen for a break before the holidays.

Jake knew the excuse she'd concocted would have to be enough for now, but word got out quick in the country and people would be asking questions. No matter the excuse, this had to be done and now. Each minute they wasted was another minute his daughter was in danger. Closing his eyes to the horror playing out in his head, Jake said his own prayer again.

After seeing her grandparents off, Ella turned back to Jake and he watched as she braced herself for what was to come.

"Let's go," she said. Then she hurried out the door before he could tell her to run, just run.

He followed behind her. "Ella, I...I should never have come here. I panicked and I'm sorry."

"You did the right thing," Ella replied, her backbone as straight as a carpenter's level. "What else could you do?

He's obviously here and he wants another go at me. Now let's get on with things."

Too late for him to stop her. Jake figured she wouldn't back down now, no matter how scared she was. But if anything happened to her, the guilt that swirled inside his gut would become an even heavier burden on his heart.

He'd have to do his best not only to save his daughter, but this time he needed to keep Ella safe, too.

Ella was headed to her old, beat-up pickup when Jake stopped her. "Let's take mine."

Frowning, she turned to his vehicle. "Don't like my driving?"

"I'd feel better taking my truck."

Ella didn't believe that but she followed him to his vehicle. She tossed her rucksack in the jump seat but held her rifle close. "Do you think he's watching my house, Jake? That maybe he's put something in my truck?"

Jake nodded. "He has to know you're here. He wanted me to come to you and I played right into his hands. I should get you to a safe place and take care of this myself."

"Don't go doubting yourself now," she said, her hand on his arm. The touch of her fingers on his skin singed her enough to make her draw back. "I want to help. I need to help."

She pointed at her old Chevy. "Let's check a few spots around here before we go off on a wild goose chase."

Jake couldn't argue with that. Her truck didn't have any hidden notes or clues. It might be old, but Ella kept it clean as a whistle. Next, they checked the barn, making sure all the animals were accounted for. Again, clean and tidy and without any sinister reminders.

"I didn't think about tending the stock," Ella said as they walked around the fenced corrals. "Maybe I can call a neighbor to help with that."

After they'd done a quick check on the perimeters of the yard and barn area, he glanced at the restaurant. "So today's Monday. It's closed?"

"Yes." Ella started that way. "I haven't even been there to check on things today." She held her rifle down and did a visual of the yard and woods.

Jake followed her with his own rifle, his gaze taking in the lighted garden path leading to a huge square pavilion-type gazebo surrounded by tall pines and bald cypress trees. It was screened in but he could see an enormous fireplace at the front of the big open building and a long wooden table with high-backed chairs centered in the space in front of the fireplace. The whole place was gussied up for a cozy Christmas. A wooden sign over the double screen doors stated, Welcome to Caddo Country.

Rustic, beautiful and isolated.

He took a long look at the nearby woods, noticing paths down to a wooden dock out over Caddo Lake.

"So…you opened a restaurant?"

Ella did the same visual, her eyes moving over the trees and then to the woods that lifted away from the shoreline.

"Yep, sorta. We cater to parties up to fifty at a time, but we like doing small groups to make it more intimate." She shrugged. "More of a meal for friends who pay than a real restaurant."

Jake gave a surprised grunt. "Never figured you for a gardener or a cook."

Her left eyebrow lifted in a graceful curve. "Because you always saw me as too ambitious to boil water?"

Jake couldn't deny it. "Yeah, maybe. What made you start doing this kind of thing?"

She got over her defensive stance pretty fast. "It happened by chance. I saw a news report about how big produce companies out in California have started doing what they call farm-to-table dinners. I tried a couple and it worked out pretty good so we expanded and now we work most of the spring and summer. Taper off a bit in the fall and winter unless it's a special request. We've got some holiday dinners planned and I'm scheduled for an open house during the upcoming Christmas Festival."

They both checked the surrounding woods and the lake again, then Jake asked a few more questions. "So it's not a 24/7 type place? More exclusive?"

She nodded. "We cook our guests a meal that comes straight off the land. The meat, the vegetables, the bread. Even the butter, cheeses and eggs. It's a real, home-cooked organic dinner and it makes people appreciate farming and growing food a whole lot more."

Impressed, Jake said, "Sounds like a lot of work."

"It is," she said over her shoulder when they reached the double wooden-faced screen doors. Pulling out a key she unlocked the bolt. "I don't know why I lock it. Anyone could cut through these screens even if they are heavy-duty weight."

"Any alarms?" Jake asked, quiet now.

"Just Zip's barking. But we do have floodlights at night and we really don't keep anything out here but cooking utensils and dishes. We have an outdoor kitchen behind the fireplace and a storage freezer back up the hill."

She pointed to a covered catwalk from the storage freezer to the open-air kitchen tucked behind the fireplace.

Jake followed her inside the wide square structure, the scents of fresh evergreen branches merging with something that smelled like cinnamon and apple pie. The big candles lining the mantel, maybe?

"Pretty place." He could see how patrons would be drawn to this spot. Homey and inviting, it boasted gleaming wooden beams and arches with heavy wooden supports between the screens. The windows provided a perfect view of the lake from every corner.

"My grandpa helped me design and build it," she said on a soft tone. "I used the life insurance money I got… after my parents passed. Took us over a year to get everything together but we've had a successful couple of seasons. As I explained, we do winter meals on request, but for the most part we shut down in early November and don't open back up until spring."

Jake followed her toward the fireplace. "Everything looks okay for now."

Ella stopped in front of the rock-covered structure. "Not everything." She pointed inside the blackened bricks of the hearth to a white piece of paper sticking up out of an iron cooking pot held by a heavy shepherd's hook.

The killer's next clue.

FOUR

"The next note," Ella said on a burst of breath. "This is real, Jake. He's come back."

Jake grabbed her hand and held it there between them. "Maybe he never left."

Ella retreated from him and went to a storage cabinet. She pulled out a set of serving tongs and used them to lift out the stiff paper. Turning, she dropped it on the polished plank table so they could read it.

"Let the games begin. It's been too long, way too long."

Jake hit his hand on a chair. "He was here. No telling how long he's been watching this place."

"I never told him I was from East Texas," Ella said, panic rising like bile in her throat. "But he somehow knew and that's why he brought me back here. I tried not to give him too much information when he had me. I didn't let on that I even knew these woods or this area."

But knowing her surroundings had been part of what saved her. That would have to be in her favor now, too. "When I came back here after he'd taken me, I stayed hidden away for the first few months. I should have left the state." She shook her head. "I've put my grandparents in danger. When the killings stopped and we thought he was dead, I got too complacent, too content. I should have left—"

"It's not your fault," Jake replied. "We all searched and searched. He was badly wounded but we couldn't find a trail past the water. Nothing. I always figured he'd gotten away or at least he'd died somewhere else but he's still on every Most-Wanted List I know. I never dreamed he'd be so bold as to come back." He looked off into the distance. "I should have kept searching."

"And I ought to have kept going," Ella said. "I could have gotten far away from here."

"He's the type who'd find you, anyway," Jake said, his eyes roving around the structure and the woods. "He probably knew you'd lived here as a child, and that's why he brought you back. If you'd left, he'd have found you and none of us would have been able to help." He checked the floor for footprints, touched on the ceiling-to-floor screens for cuts. "We never found a trace of him and the murders stopped."

Ella shivered at the thought of being in that madman's clutches again. She couldn't let it happen to Macey. Just knowing a killer had that child made Ella physically ill.

The wind lifted and the forest rustled. Down on the lake, a snowy egret lifted out over the water in a wild flight. What had startled the graceful white bird?

"Maybe you're right," Ella replied to Jake on a shaky whisper. "Maybe he's been hiding out in these woods for years now." Had he been watching her all that time?

"Hunters and fishermen would have seen him or at least signs of someone living out here," Jake said, probably trying to reassure her. It didn't work.

"He's too smart for that." Ella moved around, looking here and there, opening the narrow storage cabinets underneath one of the screened corners while she searched for anything to give her a real clue. "But how did he get in?" she asked, her mind recoiling from the nightmare inside her head. "I don't see how he did it."

Jake stared up at the stoned wall of the chimney. "Do you have a door on the back of this thing? A place where you can clean it from the outside?"

"Yes." She hurried to one of the two big screen doors on either side of the chimney and unhooked the inside latch. "I'll show you."

"Wait," Jake said, stepping ahead of her with his rifle raised. He did a quick search of the woods and the path down to the dock and then squinted across the lake canal to the other shore.

"All's quiet."

Ella didn't argue with him or try to rush ahead this time. Instead, she held her own gun at the ready and scanned the paths down to the lake. Nothing. The dark waters of the big lake flowed by in the same way they'd done for hundreds of years. The tall cypress trees swayed in the midday wind, their sighs revealing no secrets. Turtles lay sunning on old broken logs. Brown triple-strand straw from the towering pines dropped in hushed piles to the forest floor only to cover decades of decay and moist, deep earth. What else did these woods cover?

"We have to figure out the clue," she said, turning to Jake. "He's on the move and he's probably got Macey with him."

"Or he's left her somewhere, tied up and scared," Jake said. "Alone." He lowered his head, his expression dark and full of a helpless despair.

Hearing the crack in his deep Texas drawl made Ella want to take him in her arms and hold him. Or maybe fire a round from her rifle while she screamed at the top of her lungs.

"Here's the clean-out door," she said, refusing to give in to the clawing, slithering fingers of fear.

Jake pivoted to the left in front of her. "Did you keep it locked?"

"Yes. Just so no kids or varmints could accidentally get inside. It's a pretty big door."

"The lock's broken," Jake replied, pointing to the square black-iron door on the back of the stone chimney. "That's how he left the note."

"He usually doesn't leave any signs so the broken lock is significant," Ella pointed out, the technical facts clearing her head for a brief time. "Maybe he had to hurry and get away. What did the note say again?"

Jake stood, his eyes holding hers. "'Let the games begin. It's been too long. Way too long.'"

"What's he trying to tell us?" Ella paced in front of the clean-out door. She hated that all the horrible memories she'd tried to bury were now resurfacing like dead bones floating in water. "Way too long. Way too long."

"Does that make sense?" Jake asked, hope in each word.

"I don't know. I... It's hard to remember. I don't want to remember."

Jake was there, taking her rifle, pulling her into his arms. "I'm so sorry. I thought long and hard before coming here but I'm glad I did. I can't let him hurt Macey and I sure won't let him hurt you."

"I'm okay," she said, the warmth of his arms shielding her, comforting her, soothing her. "I'll be okay."

Jake stepped back as if he'd just realized how close they stood. "We need to stay on top of this. It's us against him and he knows I won't bring in anyone else unless he forces the issue. He's got a grudge going but so do we. It has been way too long. But we get a second chance to bring him in."

"Then that's what we'll do." She backed away and wiped her eyes. "Maybe if we take a ride...to...the last place we saw him."

Ella thought back over the clues so far. "He left a note directing you to the daisy necklace to prove that he's still alive and then he brought you to me to show he's not finished with us. That's two clues." She pushed at her bangs. "But what does this one mean?"

"Games?" Jake stared off into the woods. "Wait a minute. Didn't he take you when you were at a park? Near an old baseball field?"

Ella closed her eyes, her heart careening out of her body, her pulse roaring in her ears like a tornado over dirt. "Yes. Right across from the campgrounds on the other side of the lake. Yes."

Jake held his hands on her arms. "What else, Ella? *Way too long.* What does that mean?"

Ella gasped and put a hand to her mouth. "He told me it had taken me way too long to find him. That I was too late. Too late."

"The fourth body," Jake said, his tanned skin turning pale. "It took us way too long to find the fourth missing girl."

"She was dead," Ella said, shaking her head. "Dead when I found her off the path into the woods. Dead. And so he took me." She started shaking. "He kept telling me that over and over while he dragged me to an old van. 'Took you way too long. It's on your head, Agent Terrell. You took way too long to get here.'"

"We have to go to that park," Jake said. "Now."

Ella swallowed the scream inside her head and hurried after him. "We need to preserve the note."

Jake nodded and rushed into the screened gazebo and grabbed the white sheet, not even bothering to keep his prints off it.

But when they got to his truck, he took out his evidence kit and slid the square of paper into a fresh manila envelope and tagged it. Then he placed it in a safe compartment inside the big black case.

"I'll have to report this and give both the note and the necklace to the nearest state crime lab," he said. "I didn't tell the Tyler Police where I'd be on Caddo Lake, only that I was going to do some investigating of my own."

Ella got in and stared at the place she loved, seeing it now through the eyes of a killer. He'd been here, moving around her yard, touching things in her restaurant. Leaving her a definite message that dared her to come and find him. This farm had become her safe haven and now he'd ruined that with his evil touch.

"I'll get you," she said, her hands knuckled into tight fists, her rifle touching on her jeans. "I'll find you and I won't let you hurt another innocent young girl."

Oblivious to her pledge, Jake jumped in and cranked the truck and peeled out. "Where do we start?"

Ella pressed at her growing headache. "The park. It has to be the place. He wants us to go there for some reason."

"Maybe he's playing out how things went down with you and him five years ago."

"He won't live to see the ending this time," Ella blurted. Then she sent Jake a remorseful glance. "I'm sorry. I know the law dictates I apprehend him and bring him in and I know the Lord says I should forgive my enemies. But I'm having a hard time with that right now."

"I'm not judging," Jake replied. "He's got my daughter. My little girl. Forget what's right or wrong. I want him dead and I want to make sure he suffers before he dies."

Ella closed her eyes. "We've both got a lot of praying to do."

Jake's expression brewed like an approaching storm. "I'll pray, all right. I'll pray that I find my Macey and that this time, I'll be able to shoot him dead when I see him."

They made it across the county and to the park in record time. Caddo Lake covered a big area that straddled the state lines between Texas and Louisiana. Thousands of acres of water and wetlands that twisted and meandered into bayous and swamps lay before them. But Ella remembered how single-minded Jake could be when he had his teeth into a case and now he was a father on a desperate mission. A father trying to save his only child.

How would they ever manage to do that in this vast expanse of woods and water?

She took covert glances over at him, thinking age and maturity looked good on Jake Cavanaugh. He was tall and lanky with a loose-limbed kind of gait that always drew feminine sighs. He had the look of aged leather and sharp spurs, his golden-brown hair too shaggy, his tan hat broken and worn down into a perfect fit across his broad forehead. Right now, his five-o'clock shadow only added to the dark, worry-streaked scowl on his face.

Jake, back in her life. The nightmare starting all over again. Macey missing and with a psychopath. It was too much to comprehend.

But she had to absorb all of it, for Macey's sake.

For Jake's sake.

This morning, her life had been perfectly mundane and ordinary, her quiet, busy everyday routine carrying her from sleep to sleep, her weary muscles and bones toughening and strengthening with each step.

This morning, she'd been so close to a peaceful acceptance.

And then he'd come walking back into her life.

The man she'd loved for so many years.

The man she'd left behind because duty and ambition had propelled her out of control. But Jake had saved her, not just from a killer, but from herself. He'd saved her and then he'd walked away again because she was too fragile and broken to see what she had right there in front of her. She'd lost a second chance with a good man.

The man who'd come to her for help with the one thing she'd tried so hard to forget.

The Dead Drop Killer.

"Any idea where he kept you?"

"I don't remember," she replied. "I rarely saw the light of day." She shrugged. "When I ran away, I looked back and saw a dark building. A cabin maybe?"

Jake nodded. "I've got people searching for any vacant cabins or fishing camps."

Ella saw Jake looking past her and off to the right.

They'd reached the park. It was now overgrown and abandoned, a place of haunting memories and nightmare dreams. Rusty swings twisted in the wind, the old chains clinking like tattered bones. The merry-go-round squeaked against the unseen push of air, fighting the memories of laughing children.

Ella fought against those same memories. But they wrapped around her and stifled her in the same way that the gag and the blindfold the killer had placed on her had done. She remembered opening her eyes to the horror of his hideous mask after he'd jerked the blindfold off her face. Remembered thinking she'd never see her dear, sweet grandparents again.

She'd promised them this morning that she'd be careful, that she'd return to them. But first she had to expose her mind to the memories and the nightmares and the buried, hidden things.

Dear God, I don't think I can do this. I don't know what to do.

She opened her eyes and saw Jake staring at her.

"You don't have to do this," he said. "I'll track him and I'll take care of him."

"No," she said, gaining strength because she hated to witness his pain. "No. I can't let you do this alone, Jake. I won't let you go without me. We have to find Macey."

Jake leaned over and touched a rough-edged finger to her cheek. "You're the only one I knew I could trust."

"Let's search the playground and the woods," she said after she opened the truck door. Then she turned back to him, the rasp of his roughness still soft on her skin. "But Jake, sooner or later, we'll have to call for help. We might not be able to do this without a team."

"I know," he replied. "But I'm afraid he'll kill her either way. He's not only holding my girl hostage. He's got both of us in a choke hold, too. So…I have to go after him."

Ella got out of the truck and took a deep breath, then looked up at the beautiful blue sky. "Lord, we aren't really alone. You're here. I can feel You. Let that poor scared girl hear You, too. Please."

But the next thing Ella heard was a heart-stopping scream coming from deep inside the woods.

FIVE

Jake and Ella both drew their firearms and headed into the woods. An old walking trail veered off to the right. Ella motioned to Jake and they hurried up the trail.

Ella could hear footsteps hitting the solid dirt around the next curve. She jogged to get a closer look, all the while doing a visual of the surrounding woods.

Jake trotted up behind her. "Slow down. Don't get yourself killed."

She shot him a quick over-the-shoulder glance then motioned to a woman running away. "I'm going after her."

The woman was slender and tall and in good shape by the way she'd sprinted up the path. She wore a light gray jogging suit and had a lightweight scarf wrapped around her neck.

"I'm with you." Jake whirled around Ella. "Let's follow her and see where she goes."

The woman whirled around, her breath coming in gulps, her eyes going wide. When she saw Jake's gun, she panicked and looked around as if searching for a way to escape. She had red hair and a freckled face that showed she was older than they'd realized.

She hurried toward them. "Did you see him?"

"See who?" Ella called as she met up with the woman.

"A man." The woman pointed behind them. "He...he

knocked me down and then he ran away." She brushed at her jogging pants.

Jake saw a tear in her dark pants and blood running from her leg. "Are you hurt?"

"Just a skinned knee. He came out of the woods and scared me to death." She eyed their guns, her green eyes going dark. "Are you after him?"

Jake tapped his shirt pocket with a finger on his badge. "Texas Ranger. We heard a scream." Without elaborating, he started running backward. "I'll check the immediate area."

Ella watched him hurrying away, a prayer for his safety moving through her own fears. "Did you get a good look at him?" Ella asked the woman, her gun down now.

The buff woman looked frightened and skeptical, her gaze darting toward Ella. She pushed a hand through her short, damp hair. "I… Uh…" Then she let out a breath. "Oh, my, I only saw him running away and he was wearing all black, with a hoodie covering his face. He came charging out onto the path in front of me, pushed me down and ran. Scared me so badly, I let out a scream." She shivered, her hands tight against her stomach. "He went one way and I went another. I just wanted to get back home."

Ella made sure she kept checking the woods in all directions. Even in stark winter, these woods were still dense. "So you're out here alone a lot?" she asked the frightened woman. She watched the woman for signs of lying but the lady seemed genuinely surprised and scared.

The jogger nodded, her eyes full of questions, her expression earnest and curious. "I've been walking and jogging this trail since we moved here about five years ago. Never had a problem before."

Five years ago. Had this woman moved in right after Ella had been found? Maybe she had no idea what had happened in these woods or maybe she knew everything.

Ella glanced around, hoping to see Jake, and then looked back at the woman. "It's a mighty isolated area."

The woman gulped another breath. "Yes, but I'm careful. I live not far up the path. On the lake." She patted the pocket of her lightweight jacket. "I have pepper spray but he came out of nowhere. Didn't have time to grab it."

Wishing the lady had been able to spray the man in the face, Ella nodded and stepped closer. "We're looking for someone. The man who ran past you could be a very dangerous criminal. Are you sure you didn't get a look at his face?"

"I'm sorry, but no." The woman shivered as the biting wind picked up. "I usually don't see that many people out here, but today I'm glad you two came along. He could have come back and chased me or worse."

"Can you describe the man's clothing again?" Ella asked, her throat tightening. "His height maybe?"

The woman squinted and pursed her lips. "He was tall, medium build, and like I said before, he was wearing black sweats and a black hoodie pulled up over his head. He ran right past me with a grunt but he had his head down." She blew air up toward her damp bangs. "Should I be concerned?"

"You should be cautious," Ella replied. "You might want to cut back on your jogging schedule for the next week or so."

"Not a problem," the woman said. "I like my solitude but I don't want to be in the woods with anyone dangerous." She stared out into the trees. "This place is usually so peaceful and quiet, not much happens out here."

Ella tried to focus on getting information but she worried about Jake with each breath. Why wasn't he back?

"Have you seen anything else unusual along the trail in the last few days?" she asked.

The woman shook her head and did a slow march in

place. "No, but I'll sure be on the lookout from now on. I'll get my exercise at home for a while."

After a few more questions, Ella took down the woman's name and phone number and gave her Jake's name as a contact. "Thank you, Mrs. Parsons. We'll file this report for now. If you notice anything out of the ordinary, will you give us a call?"

"Of course. Thanks for the warning." The woman pivoted back the way she'd been running. "Am I safe to get home? It's only about a quarter of a mile."

Ella eyeballed the woods. "Maybe we can give you a lift."

She pulled out her cell and called Jake, hoping he'd silenced his phone at least.

Before she heard a ring, he came around the curve, his face set in a grim line that told her nothing. She didn't ask if he'd found anything. The less Mrs. Parsons heard or saw the better off she'd be.

"Everyone okay here?" he asked, his tone calm, his face a blank wall.

"We're fine. This is Maria Parsons. She lives up around the curve."

Jake slanted his gaze toward the slim woman. "Thanks for your help. I didn't find anyone."

"It's the strangest thing," Maria Parsons said. "Just popped up outta the blue."

Jake gave Ella a scowl and a stare. "Let's get Mrs. Parsons home safely."

He wanted them out of these woods, Ella realized. And he probably wanted to get a look at where this woman lived.

Because she might have just seen the Dead Drop Killer.

Jake's heart seemed to be stuck against his ribs. He couldn't say anything in front of their witness but he'd come across another note in the woods near the spot where he'd found Ella on that night five years ago.

"Is there something you're not telling me?" Mrs. Parsons asked from the passenger's-side seat. "If we're in danger around here, we need to know."

"No danger yet," Ella said from her perch in the jump seat behind the woman. "We just have to follow every lead. You know how it is with the Rangers. They track people all over the state and they check every angle."

"I get that," the other woman replied. "But y'all are scaring me. What did this person do?"

"You don't need to be scared," Ella replied after Jake shot her a warning scowl through the rearview mirror. "But you do need to be aware. Carry pepper spray and always be alert by checking your surroundings. And stay off the trail for a few days."

"I doubt I'll ever feel safe here again," Mrs. Parsons replied. "I love this place, though."

"I love it, too," Ella said. "You probably have nothing to worry about. I'll make it a point to call you after we've checked around."

"I'd appreciate that," the woman said as she pointed to a long driveway. "This is my house."

Jake pulled the truck up the lane to the simple brick structure. Had Ella passed this house the night she was taken?

"Do you live alone?" he asked, his heart pounding. Taking in a deep breath, he held his growing concern at bay. His daughter was out there with a madman and the longer they delayed, the worse things could become.

"Yes. Widowed. But I have an alarm."

"Good," Jake replied. "Be careful and be aware."

"Thanks." Mrs. Parsons got out of the truck then turned with a hand on the door. Her green eyes settled on Ella.

"I thought you looked familiar. I remember you from the news reports. Are you Ella Terrell?"

Ella swallowed and nodded. "Yes, ma'am."

Maria Parsons's green eyes went soft. "I heard the stories after I bought our house, but…I fell in love with this place. And…I understood…all of that was over."

Jake glanced at Ella then got out the truck to hurry the woman into the house. "Thank you for your help."

Maria Parsons kept her eyes on Ella. "Who are you looking for?"

Ella lowered her head. "I can't comment on that."

Mrs. Parsons gave her a knowing look. "I understand." Then she reached out a hand to Ella. "Whoever it is, honey, I hope you find him. I sure won't go back on that trail until you do."

Ella nodded. "I'm only helping out. I'm not here in an official capacity."

"If you've got a Ranger with you, it's official," the other woman replied, her expression full of compassion. "I'm sure it will all come out in the wash."

"I hope so." Ella gave Mrs. Parsons a direct glance. "We don't want to scare anyone so I'd appreciate you keeping this quiet for now."

Maria Parsons held her hands together, a serene expression covering her face. "I hardly ever see anyone out here."

Jake took Mrs. Parsons by the elbow. "If you do see anyone who stands out or acts strange, you need to call me." He handed her a card with his name and phone number.

Mrs. Parsons nodded and waved to Ella. Jake escorted her to the porch then checked inside the house. After reminding the woman to stay safe, he told her a whole team of investigators would soon be roaming these woods.

He couldn't do this alone and he prayed Macey would be safe until he could find her.

When he got back to the truck, he sat there staring out

into the woods for a minute. Ella got out and hopped up front, but she watched until the older woman was safe inside the house. Then Ella put her hands on the dashboard and laid her head against them.

Jake closed his eyes and kept his prayers open and urgent while Ella did her own quiet praying.

He didn't know how he was going to do this without God's help.

"Jake?"

He opened his eyes and looked over at Ella. He'd wanted to see her for so long now, but never under these circumstances. Not with his daughter out there somewhere, scared and cold and hurting.

"Did you see him?" she asked. "Did you find something?"

He cranked the truck and pulled out of Mrs. Parsons's yard.

"I didn't see him, no. But I did find the next clue."

Ella inhaled a gasp. "What is it? A note? Something else?"

He pulled a clear square bag out of his jacket pocket. "He left this, already bagged for us." Jake handed the baggie over to Ella.

She took it, stared down at it then glanced over at him.

"Precious Memories," she read from the cutout lettering at the top of the piece of paper. Then she saw the newspaper article about her.

"It's about my rescue," she whispered, a hand going to her mouth. Local FBI Agent Found Barely Alive in Woods Near Caddo Lake. The headline went on to say that an alleged serial killer might still be at large.

She stopped reading out loud, her eyes moving over the yellowed article. "He kept this all those years."

"He's still obsessed with you," Jake replied, anger fueling his need to find the man who'd taken his daughter. "You're the one who got away and he doesn't like that."

They both sat silent, trying to absorb what this meant.

"Is this it? Just this article?" Ella finally asked, her blue eyes rivaling the clear sky. "This doesn't tell us anything."

"But it does," Jake replied. "Precious Memories, remember?"

Ella put a hand to her mouth. "I sang a solo of that hymn in church one Sunday, back in high school. How did he know?"

Jake pulled up to the old park again and after shutting off the engine he turned to her. "It means he's known you for a long time and…that he probably lived around here. He might still live somewhere nearby."

"But how could he possibly be back here without someone seeing him?"

"He's been hiding in plain sight," Jake said. "No one ever saw his face. You're the only one who can identify him and all you know is the same as what Mrs. Parsons told us. He wears all black and keeps his face covered."

Ella lifted her gaze to the woods, terror washing her skin pale. "Do you think that was him out on the path?"

"Yes," Jake said, his hands gripping the steering wheel. "I think he's been watching that woman and he knew we'd show up here sooner or later. He used Maria Parsons as a distraction and as a teaser to draw us in."

"Where did you find this?" Ella asked, her finger moving over the bag.

"I found another path leading back to the playground," he told her. "And this was lying on a tree stump around the curve in the path."

"He doubled back while we were with Maria Parsons?"

Jake nodded, his stomach churning with a sick, solid fear. "Possibly. Or he dropped this once he'd scared her into screaming. He obviously wants us to go to your church."

Ella's head shot up. "I'm glad we gathered the task force and you let them search for that old camp house." Her eyes held a plea. "I know they're doing everything they can behind the scenes, but we need a lot of investigators on this. It's too much for just the two of us."

Jake couldn't argue with that. He was caught in a vise that squeezed from all directions. He wanted to find his daughter but trying to do so alone put her life in danger. But if he called in help, the killer would soon figure that out and...Jake didn't want to think what might happen.

"I'll call them," he finally said. "But we'll have to keep them at a distance while we keep following the clues."

"He wants me," Ella said. "So we have to let him think he has me." She stared out into the sun-dappled woods. "Just like last time."

Jake didn't like that idea. He wouldn't risk Ella being taken again. "I'm not letting you out of my sight. I shouldn't have done that today."

"I was with a harmless older lady," Ella retorted. Then she touched his hand. "But it's good to know you've got my back."

Jake cranked the truck. "I won't let him hurt you again and I won't let him hurt Macey."

"Then do what you have to do," Ella retorted. "And I'll do what I need to, to help you."

SIX

Ella had been attending services at the tiny Lake Chapel off and on for most of her life. As Jake pulled the truck up the gravelly drive toward the white clapboard structure, she had to wonder if the Dead Drop Killer had also been attending.

And watching her.

Staring up at the tiny bell tower and old iron steeple, Ella prayed that they could find this man soon.

"Do you think he's been here?" she asked Jake, needing to hear his reassurances. What if this was someone she knew, someone she did business with? Someone who pretended to be her friend?

Jake didn't mince words. "He's either been here off and on during the years or he heard about that hymn somewhere, somehow. Maybe when he read that news clipping the first time." He ran a hand down his beard stubble. "He could have been there the day you sang that solo."

Ella didn't want to dwell on that scenario. "We made a mistake, not verifying his death, didn't we?"

Jake turned to face her. "We searched these woods twice over and put out all kinds of warnings and descriptions. We did everything we could to locate him…but yes, we made a mistake. He got away and we got complacent."

"He was just biding his time," she replied. "But I wonder why he came back and why now."

Jake opened the truck door. "I think he came back for you and I think he took Macey because he knew you'd go after her. He knew we'd both search for her. That's a given."

Ella closed her eyes to that horror. "He's obviously been keeping tabs on you, too. He wants both of us to suffer."

"Well, guess what?" Jake got out then turned and waited for her to do the same. "It's working."

Jake did a visual of the entire churchyard and parking lot. "Do you recognize that white van?"

Ella turned to where he pointed. "Belongs to the custodian. He's worked here for years."

"We might need to question him," Jake replied.

Ella came around the truck and walked with him toward the stone steps of the chapel. The heavy cypress doors were never locked. The chapel welcomed anyone to come inside at any time and pray. Ella sure intended to do that today.

But fear gripped her like a tightening vine. What would she find in there? What was Jake thinking right now?

"I hope…" He stopped, gathered himself as he stared down at his feet. "Help me, Ella. I don't know if I can go in there. Macey—"

"I've got it," she said, stepping past him, her gun at the ready.

"No," he said, moving up the steps behind her. "I'm okay. I can't let you go in there alone."

Ella didn't argue with him. She didn't mind doing this without him but having Jake by her side gave her the kind of security that had been sorely missing from her life.

"Side by side," she said on a shattered whisper.

Jake nodded, his gaze covering her in a warm blanket of hope. Just enough hope to push at that unspoken fear clawing through her system and remind her that she was still attracted to this man.

He turned the old brass doorknob and the door creaked open with a screech of protest. Ella stepped in behind him, her eyes adjusting to the shadowy darkness, the feel of the cool, silent air hitting her in the face with the scent of lemony furniture polish and old wood. A familiar, soothing smell in a comforting, peaceful place. The stained-glass windows that usually brought her peace now glistened with prisms of light, forcing her to blink and refocus.

Bracing herself, she gazed up the aisle toward the altar. The pine prayer bench with the open Bible lying on top hadn't changed. The offering plates were in their spots beside the Bible. The pulpit was intact on one side of the altar and the tiny choir loft was on the other side.

At first glance, everything seemed secure and serene, as untouched and pure as this sacred spot had been all of her life.

And then she saw it.

"Jake?" she said on a caught whisper. "Jake?"

Something on the floor, protruding out from behind the pulpit.

"I see," he said, his reply husky and scraping. "C'mon."

He took her hand, an unusual move for a man who held his emotions inside like a rock levee holding back a river.

Ella prayed, gulped in a breath, prayed some more. *Please, Lord, no. Don't let that be—*

"It's…it's Macey's sweater," Jake said, his own breath heaving. He let go of Ella's hand and stepped to the left side of the altar where the minister's chair was located.

Ella hurried after him, her gaze hitting on the pretty blue button-up sweater lying stretched on the floor. Jake didn't pick it up at first. He just stood there staring at it. Ella took a couple of photos with her phone then used the muzzle of her gun to lift the lightweight sweater. "I don't see anything—"

"There," Jake said, pointing to one sleeve.

Ella studied the garment. There. A drop of what looked like blood, near the left arm cuff. Holding her phone with her other hand, she snapped a shot of the dark stain.

"We need to get this to the crime scene techs," she said. "Along with my necklace and the notes we have so far."

Jake nodded, swallowed. "She was wearing this last time I saw her. She left for the mall, going to buy a dress. She wanted something pretty for Luke. A good boy. A nice boy." He stopped and stared at the sweater.

Jake went back over the details as if he couldn't believe what he'd seen and heard. But Ella knew he wasn't processing this for evidence. Right now, he was a father who was worried about his daughter. She could only imagine the horrible images he must be creating in his mind. She'd lived some of that horror. Her heart tore open, thinking of what Macey must be going through.

We're here. We're coming to find you.

"We'll find her, Jake. I promise."

Jake didn't answer. "I need to get an evidence bag outta the truck."

"Let me," Ella replied. She carefully laid the sweater back against the big wooden chair. "Stay here. I'll hurry."

Then she turned and trotted over the old red carpet on the aisle, her footfalls sneaking after her like shadows chasing at her heels.

When Ella got outside, she made sure to absorb her surroundings. The church grounds and the woods were silent, the old familiar wooden nativity scene soothing her nerves. She glanced at the old cemetery where her parents were buried and where her grandparents would be buried one day. Did she want to be there, too? Not just yet.

"Precious memories," she whispered, wondering what

message the psycho was trying to send this time. "Unseen angels." She tried to remember all the words to the old hymn. "Sacred scenes unfold...echoes of the past..."

Nothing came to her, but she did feel the past echoing out over these woods. The tombstones and old oaks looked just as still and serene as the rest of this place. Faded artificial flowers stood in stiff, lifeless lines against the rows of monuments, reminding her of the forgotten memories she tried to keep hidden away. The wind tickled at her skin then spilled over her, taking its secrets with it.

Ella headed to the truck and found Jake's evidence kit then located a large paper bag. She was halfway back to the chapel when she heard it.

"Ella?"

Her name, drawn out on the chilly wind that rustled through the trees. "Ella, help me."

Ella whirled around. "Macey?"

She squinted into the dense woods. The wind picked up, causing the tall pines to shake and sway. Somewhere deep in the woods, she heard a rustling sound, like someone running away.

"Who's there?" Ella drew her gun again and strained to hear. She didn't dare go into those woods alone.

"Ella, please!"

"Macey?" Dropping the evidence bag, Ella ran toward the chapel. "Macey, we're here. We'll find you."

The doors burst open and Jake leapt over the steps. "I heard you calling her? Did you see her?"

The hope on his face broke Ella's heart. She shook her head. "I...I thought I heard her calling me from the woods."

Jake started that way, but Ella grabbed his arm. "I think it's a trick. I think he's out there but...I don't think he has Macey with him." If he did, he wouldn't let them see her.

Jake stalked away. "Macey? Macey, it's Daddy. Honey,

can you hear me?" He turned to Ella. "But you said you heard her, right?"

"I thought I heard her. I can't be sure."

"I have to go investigate," he said. "Ella, I have to."

Ella nodded. "I'll go bag the sweater."

"No," Jake replied, taking her by the arm. "In my sight at all times, okay?"

Ella nodded and followed him toward the tree line. Their approach caused a covey of quails to flutter into the air, startling them both into action.

Jake held his gun out, then let out a breath. Ella did the same. "We should call for backup," she suggested.

"The task force is setting up at your place," he explained. "I called them from inside while you went to get the evidence bag." He gave her a solemn gaze. "He won't come back there. It's too public a place. I'll send someone to look for the cabin where you think he held you."

"If it's still there," she replied, worried that the suspect would take Macey somewhere else. "But you and me, Jake. We need to be extra careful. He's watching. He knows we're out here on our own."

"He has Macey and he's trying to keep her—and us—isolated," Jake said, gritting out each word.

"Daddy!"

The scream pierced the woods and echoed against the pure white of the old chapel's sturdy walls.

Jake took off into the woods, his gun raised.

Ella had no choice but to rush in after him.

Jake's heart trumpeted against his chest like a caught bird chirping to break free. He couldn't breathe, couldn't take in air. The hurt of knowing his daughter was in danger almost brought him to his knees. But he had to keep moving and he had to stay on target. He'd never wanted to kill another human being.

Until now.

"Jake, be careful."

He could hear Ella's warning inside the drum of his pulse, the words ringing in his ears as if coming through a tunnel.

"Macey?" He stopped in a copse of wiry shrubs, caught his held breath and waited.

A soft rustling to the left.

He turned that way, Ella on his heels. "Macey? It's Daddy. Can you hear me, honey?"

Nothing.

And then, footfalls running away.

Jake took off toward the sound, his mind boiling over with every dark reality he'd ever witnessed on this job.

Not Macey, Lord. Not my little girl. Please, dear God, protect her.

The footfalls drifted away in one last laughing echo and then the woods went quiet again.

Jake stood between two twisted live oaks, in a clearing surrounded by scrub oaks and saplings. He circled the area, his gaze alert for any movement. "Macey?"

No answer. Nothing.

He fell to his knees. "Macey, it's Daddy. Please answer me."

No answer.

"Jake?"

He turned, still on his knees, to find Ella standing there with a small black box in her hand. "What is that?"

She kneeled down beside him. "A tape recorder. I saw it by that big oak over there." She hit a button.

"Ella, help me. Please."

Jake covered his face with his hand. "It's her. It's Macey."

They listened to Macey's voice calling to them over and over in a recorded loop.

"She's scared, Ella. She's so scared." Jake sank back then lowered his head. "I have to find her."

Ella nodded and gently placed the recorder on the dusty ground. "He left this here for us to hear. Left it and then ran away."

Jake stared at Ella and saw the fear and the resolve in her sky-blue eyes. And the tears. Pushing at the moisture in his own eyes, he focused on the woman he'd never stopped loving. If anyone could help him find Macey, it would be Ella. She was the bravest, strongest woman he'd ever known.

Ella stared back at him, the unspoken things between them lingering in the air like a soft mist. And then she pulled him into her arms and held him close while he cried.

Two hours later, the sun was beginning to set out over the dark lake. Jake pulled the pickup into Ella's driveway and saw a line of unmarked cars in the graveled parking lot that usually served as restaurant parking.

They hadn't gotten very far on their own.

"I suggested this, but I'm surprised you agreed to put the command post here," Ella said, her voice sounding as drained as Jake felt.

He stared up at the house. "When I saw the sweater, I knew we had to bring in backup or we'd be chasing through the woods all night and maybe for a long time to come. He'd be crazy to try anything with all of us here, guarding the place."

"But he has been here."

Jake lifted his chin. "And he won't dare come back. He has to know we can't keep this a secret." He motioned to the cars. "I'm hoping he'll think you're open for business, but he has ways of figuring out our next move."

"Are you thinking this will cause him to leave another clue somewhere?"

"I hope," Jake replied. "Honestly, I don't know what to do next. He managed to hide his tracks—again."

He regretted breaking down out there in the woods, but he didn't regret holding Ella tight against him. So tight he could hear her heartbeat in time with his own. That had given Jake the strength to get up and keep moving. But the few tracks they found were hard to decipher in this dry winter weather. Mostly just broken twigs and a few dusty partial prints of what looked like clean-bottomed shoes. Moccasins maybe?

It didn't matter. They'd tracked him back out of the woods behind the church. Nothing. Not even the next clue. He'd somehow circled back around and gotten away. Again.

They'd questioned the church custodian but the man was partially deaf and walked with a limp. He was retired Army and only worked part-time. He didn't have a clue as to what they were talking about and kept telling them he'd been the only one on the property all morning and that he'd been in the adjacent education building for most of that time. They could rule him out, along with the minister and the church secretary.

"Do you think—?"

Jake shook his head. "Do I think he'll kill her?" He glanced over at Ella. "I'm going on his usual MO, Ella. He's killed all of them."

"Except me," she reminded him. "Macey sounds like a smart girl. If she can find a way to escape, she will."

"And what if he catches her and kills her, anyway?"

"I don't know," Ella replied. "But we can't give up, Jake. We can't stop. We have to try and figure out what might be next."

She opened the door and gathered all of the bagged evidence. "Let's get this processed. We could get lucky and find some of the killer's DNA."

Jake's expression darkened. "I doubt that. He's too smart to let us find any trace of him. That's the reason we've never caught him to begin with."

Two members of the task force had found an abandoned camp house near the park but after searching the rickety cabin from top to bottom, they'd reported back with nothing. No trace of anyone living there or hiding there. No trace of his daughter.

He wished he'd stayed with this case five years ago. But after months of verifying dead-end leads and searching these woods, sometimes on his off time, Jake had finally gone back to his other cases and his young daughter. He had to take care of Macey after her mother died. His parents helped with Macey before their deaths and her other grandparents lived in Georgia. She'd been his responsibility and he'd failed her. Couple that with Ella's rejection of him yet again and he'd just gone on with his life. The irony of it was if he'd kept searching, Macey might not be out there with a killer right now.

He closed his eyes and willed the darkness to recede. He had to keep the faith. That's what his parents would tell him.

That's what Macey would tell him.

"Jake, let's get inside. I'll be glad to open up the dining hall for the task force."

Jake looked across at Ella. "That might be good. Let's try to keep things normal. Maybe think about bringing in some of your workers."

"Sure." She nodded. "I have to feed the animals right now but I'll get someone else to do that for the rest of the week."

"Need some help?"

"No." She managed a weak smile then motioned toward the house. "You take care of reading in the team and I'll take care of feeding the team after I get the animals settled. And I'll be glad to answer any questions when I report in, too."

Jake gave her his own version of a smile. "I'll send a man out to the stables with you."

"Okay."

They went toward the house and found a half-dozen law officers waiting on the big back porch.

"Door's locked," one of the men explained with a tight smile. Then he turned serious. "We've checked out the woods and the outbuildings. All clear."

Jake introduced the hefty gray-haired sheriff to Ella. "Ella, this is Sheriff Doug Steward. He grew up on the other side of the lake. He'll be in charge of the task force but the Tyler Police will be part of the team, too, since Macey was taken in Tyler."

"Nice to meet you," Ella said to the robust sheriff, her voice strained.

"Not under these circumstances," Doug replied. He shook Ella's hand and then gave Jake a long stare. "How you holding up?"

"Not too good," Jake admitted. He took the bottled water someone handed him. "What have y'all got so far?"

"Not much," the sheriff admitted. "Let's get inside and we'll set up and update you. We got a top-notch team with members from the local FBI, too. Everybody wants in on this one."

Ella motioned from the door. "I'll feed y'all down at the dining hall after we all report. First, I have to tend the animals."

Jake turned to the sheriff. "Send someone with her."

The sheriff motioned to a plainclothes deputy. "Ralph, escort Miss Terrell to the barn, please."

Ralph, young and dark-haired, nodded and introduced himself to Ella. "Let's go, ma'am."

"Call me Ella," she said, her gaze slipping over Jake. "I have a feeling we'll all be in this for the long haul."

Jake watched as the two walked away, their voices carrying over the sloping yard. Ella would brief the young deputy.

Meantime, he went about filling in the blanks for the rest of the team. After thirty minutes had passed, he heard static on the sheriff's radio.

"Sir, you need to get down to the barn and stables," Ralph said over the wire. "We got a problem down here."

Jake didn't wait to hear. He was out the door before the sheriff could summon the rest of the team.

SEVEN

Ella heard Jake calling her name.

"In here," she called back from the corner of the long, deep stable and barn. She shot a glance at the stunned deputy standing beside her. He'd probably never seen anything like this.

Jake rushed through the stable, his gaze locking with Ella's. "What is it?"

"Our next clue," she said, her voice shaky. She swallowed and tried to regain control. Then she pointed to the wall. A message written in white paint stated: Bad decision.

Jake read the message, his eyes moving down to the limp body of a baby goat.

The deputy shook his head. "Found him after we'd fed and watered the goats and the cows."

Ella gave him a grateful glance. "I realized the runt kid was missing but figured he'd show up if I kept calling. The horses were restless, so I came back in to check them and feed them. That's when I found this poor little fellow." She let out a dry sob. "He broke its neck."

Jake's expression went cold with dread and disgust. "I guess I was wrong about him not coming back here."

"He had to have done it while we were gone all day," Ella replied, her hand on Jake's arm. "It's just another way of tormenting us." She hated to show him the note but it couldn't be helped.

But Jake was already thinking ahead. His expression had now turned dark and grim. "Any other explanations?"

Ella pointed to the nearest stall. "He left us an extra message along with the one on the wall. We found this note tucked in between the stall boards."

Jake let out a grunt as he read the words on the torn white paper. "'The one lamb thou shalt offer in the morning.'"

Deputy Ralph cleared his throat. "I looked it up, sir. It's from Exodus."

Jake closed his eyes and pinched his nose with his thumb and forefinger. "And what is the rest of the verse?"

Ralph glanced at Ella and she nodded. "Go ahead."

"'And the other lamb thou shalt offer at even.'"

Jake kicked at the nearest stall. "Is he saying my daughter will be the evening lamb? The second sacrifice?"

The deputy shifted on his heels to answer his phone. "I don't know." Turning back to Jake, he said, "We just got a text from the Tyler Police. Luke Hurst didn't show up for school today."

Jake glared at the deputy. "Luke? That's Macey's boyfriend." He flipped his gaze back to Ella. "Do you think he did something to Luke, too?"

Ella touched his arm again. "He's messing with us, Jake. You know he is. As long as we follow the clues, we have a chance of keeping her alive. Maybe Luke's out searching for her."

Jake gave her a look that scared her. "He did this because I brought in the task force. You know it and I know it. He told me to come alone and we brought in these people. He's probably killed both of them."

"After the first dead drop we didn't have a choice," Ella reminded him. "He had to figure you'd bring in help."

Jake placed his hands on the planked stall and pressed against the faded wood until Ella imagined splinters were piercing his palms. He held his head down. "What if we're too late already? What if he's already killed her and Luke?"

"We have to hold out hope," Ella replied, but when she glanced around, none of the men listening to her seemed to have any expressions of hope. "We have to keep at it so we can find her. The task force will look for Luke."

Jake whirled to glare at her. "And where do we go from here?"

Sheriff Steward stepped close to Jake. "We start with the evidence. We follow the trail. We put our heads together and come up with a plan." He paused then gave Jake an imploring stare. "Man, you're the best at this stuff. Think with your head, for your daughter's sake."

Jake inhaled a breath. "I don't have any other choice, so let's get busy."

He stared over at Ella, his eyes going a burnished gold. "The other girls usually died within a week of being taken."

"Then we have four days left," she said, urging him away from the dead kid. "Let's get to the house and I'll fix some sandwiches. We'll put our heads together and figure this out."

Jake nodded, but the stress of the long night and this day showed on the slashes of strain shadowing his face.

The deputy walked along with Ella. "Should I bury the little goat, ma'am?"

Ella shook her head. "Thank you, but you need to work with the forensic team to gather any evidence you can find. Take pictures and ask the team to do a video. Then swab it, starting with the head and neck. We need to bag him and put him in one of the coolers until we can get a veterinarian to do an autopsy. Make sure you and one of the others do a thorough search of the area, take lots of pictures, dust for prints and record everything. Check his fur for any human hair or anything—clothing fibers or human epidermis. That poor little creature is now part of a crime scene."

Ella called her grandparents to update and reassure them and she also called several of her staff members to give them a general overview of the situation. *General* being that a dangerous criminal could be in the area and the local law enforcement had taken over the farm. That would have to do for now. But as soon as the media got wind of this situation, things would get crazy.

So now she focused on what she did best these days. She cooked for the people gathered here to help Jake find his daughter. With officers from several different law enforcement agencies gathered here, she should feel safe. But she couldn't shake her fears unless she looked into Jake's eyes.

Even though the dining hall was basically a big screened-in porch, the task force members agreed that for now it would make a good command center. It had the fireplace for heat and hookup for computers and phones and lots of tables and chairs to spread out maps and discuss strategy. They'd started a whiteboard to keep up with the particulars, especially the dead drop clues.

Ella had to wonder about how they would go about this. Old habits came back as she chopped vegetables for soup and sliced freshly baked bread for sandwiches made with country ham and ripe, red tomatoes covered with her own spicy dressing. This busywork helped to calm her while she thought back over this day and everything that had happened.

It seemed like a lifetime since Jake had walked into the barn this morning.

When she'd been with the FBI, she'd often gone home to her Dallas apartment and cooked everything from cookies and cakes to casseroles and stews. Then she'd take the food to neighbors and coworkers since she could never eat all of it, living alone.

Funny, on those nights after a long day on the job, with some days worse than others, she'd often think about what her life would have been like if she'd stayed here on the lake and married Jake right out of high school. They'd be living in Tyler or maybe near the lake and she would have cooked for him every night and by now, they would have had at least two children, maybe three.

It's almost too late for us now.

They'd both aged into their mid-thirties. They'd both had life-changing events happen to them. And now? *Why is this happening again, Lord? Why did he let me live for an extra week? What does he want from me?*

Ella prayed and chopped, wondered and prepared. Had the Dead Drop Killer allowed her to escape so he could get away, too? Had he come back again to finish the job?

"That smells good."

She jumped and whirled around to find Jake standing inside the big, industrial kitchen at the back of the restaurant. "Oh, hi."

"I didn't mean to scare you," he said as he sauntered closer. "Just wanted to check on you."

Ella gave him a soft smile. "I have two guards, one at each door."

"I know that, but…" He stopped and stared out into the dark night. "Okay, they ran me out. Sheriff Steward says I need to take a break and let them do their jobs."

Ella smiled again, while her heart broke. "He's got a point. You're too wound-up and worried to think straight."

Jake grunted, his fingers tapping against the tiled counter. "I'm a Texas Ranger. I always think straight."

"Not this time, cowboy. And it's understandable."

He ran a hand over his already-tousled hair. "They're

going to send out teams to all the drop sites to see if I missed anything. Which I probably did."

"They'll be able to look with an objective eye," Ella replied, her FBI brain churning. "So that's good. And that's why it's so important to bring in a team."

"Not if it puts her in danger, though."

What could she say to that? Macey was in danger, but Ella's gut told her the girl was still alive. Her prayers lifted again as she asked God to show them the way. "We need all the eyes we can find for this one, Jake. He might be angry but he won't give up the game just yet."

"It's not a game."

"No, not to us. But it is to him. So we have to treat it like a game, whether we like it or not."

Jake's low growl rumbled into the air. "I hate this. Hate it. I had to call Luke's folks and try to comfort them while I tried to get information from them but I've never felt so helpless. First Macey and now Luke—missing."

She cut off a chunk of bread and slapped some butter on it. "Eat this."

Jake took the bread and held it, his eyes not really seeing it at all. Then he brought it to his mouth and bit into it. After chewing for a minute, he placed the bread on a napkin. "Good."

Ella wiped her hands on a clean dishcloth. "But you don't have an appetite."

"No."

She fought for something to say and finally gave in to the one thing on his mind. His little girl. "You were… maybe nineteen when Macey was born?"

His smile showed the strain and the relief. "Yes. Too young to raise a kid but…Natalie wanted a baby."

Ella's heart took the little stab that remark brought. "Natalie was a pretty girl. A beautiful woman."

Jake lifted his head and gave Ella a look that said a lot but told her nothing. "Yeah. She died way too young."

"And I'm sorry for that." Ella stirred the tomato-basil soup, then dropped a sprig of rosemary into the bright burnt-orange liquid. "What's Macey like?"

He grinned before he remembered his grief. "She's a lot like her mama. Dark hair and brown eyes. A big smile. Sassy and smart." His cougar eyes turned golden. "She has my temper and my stubborn streak."

Ella remembered those traits in him. She started putting together the sandwiches and before she could ask him anything else, Jake stepped up to the counter and began helping her. He passed bread slices slathered with the spicy dressing so she could cover them with the sliced ham and fresh tomatoes. Soon they had a system going as they worked side by side, a system that kept their silent screams at bay while they performed this mundane task.

When they were finally finished, Ella stopped and turned to him. "Ready to eat a bite now?"

Jake nodded. "I guess I need to put something besides coffee on my stomach."

"Yes. I think that's a very good idea."

He didn't move, however. He just stood there, staring out into the woods. "I…I had to give them a picture of her…you know…for the Amber Alert."

"I know. You wanted to keep this secret to protect her, but you also realized you had to get help wherever you could. He knows all of that, Jake. He's using Macey to get to us. He needs her to keep us guessing."

Jake let go of the fragile control he'd held back since they'd returned. "What if he gets tired of playing this sick game, Ella? What then?"

Ella couldn't answer that question. "I don't know. We just have to keep praying and we have to keep working on figuring this out." She touched a hand to his arm, her heart wanting to comfort him while her head told her to hold back. "Don't give up, Jake. We have a long road ahead of us. This time, we'll catch him and he won't ever hurt anyone again."

Jake grabbed Ella close, startling her. But his hands on her arms were gentle and shaking. "Can you promise me that? Can you?"

"No, I can't," Ella replied. "But I can promise you I'll do my best to reach that end."

His eyes washed over her with a helplessness that brought tears to her eyes. "I want to believe that and I'm trying to pray, but I keep asking God why he's putting my little girl through this. It was bad enough when that madman had you, Ella. But now…"

He didn't finish. He dropped his hands and walked away. "I'll tell 'em it's ready," he said over his shoulder.

But Ella saw the weight of the world on his broad shoulders. Jake Cavanaugh was a proud, brave man and one of the best Rangers in Texas. If he ever did find the Dead Drop Killer, nobody would be able to stop him from killing the man with his bare hands.

"And he'll have to get in line behind me," Ella whispered to the shadows. Then after going over her day again in her head, she added a small prayer. "Lord, help us all."

EIGHT

Jake woke with a start. Blinking, he remembered where he was and why he was here. That brought him up off the couch, his bare feet fighting against the light blanket Ella had given him earlier. Still in his rumpled clothes, he sat taking in air.

He'd dreamed of Macey. She'd been younger, running along the water's edge with her mother. They were laughing, happy, carefree.

Now, here in the darkness, he had to remember where Macey was tonight. Jake sat staring at the stream of moonlight that filtered through the farmhouse windows. A beautiful harvest moon grinned down on the entire house but the dancing shadows from the trees moved through the room like black lace.

He wanted to run out into those dark, dense woods and shout to the world that he needed his little girl back.

Please, Lord, bring her back to me.

The sheer helplessness of his situation made him antsy and disoriented. What could he do but put one foot in front of the other and keep doing his job? But this waiting and watching was going to kill him.

No. You have to stay strong for Macey and for Ella.

Outside, guards patrolled in that moonlight, to keep Ella safe. He refused to leave her here alone.

Now, he got up and walked the length of the big living room, memories of the many meals he'd shared in this house bringing a small bit of comfort. And a large dose of regret.

Ella's parents had died in a head-on collision out on the interstate just after her fifteenth birthday. Her grandparents had immediately taken her in and raised her through her teen years. He'd been around for most of those years, too.

Until his mule-headed logic had backfired on him and Ella had told him to get lost.

"Why can't we both have careers in law enforcement? You've known me for years, Jake. And you also know that after my daddy died, I decided I wanted to work for the FBI—just like him."

He could still hear her voice, see the disappointment in her pretty blue eyes. But Jake had always believed she'd only chosen that field because of a misguided sense of duty and maybe to keep her memories of her daddy close.

So he'd argued against it. "I thought we'd both stay here on the lake. Raise our kids here. I mean, I'll work hard and you can find something around here. Why would you want to leave?"

"You've never listened to me, Jake. I want to work for the FBI. I want to be an agent. I…I have to do this, for my father. He was a good agent but he died too young. I want to make him proud. I'm not kidding about that."

Jake could certainly understand wanting to make someone proud. "But your daddy was proud of you already. He doesn't care if you work for the FBI or not. He'd want you to be happy."

"I will be happy. I will."

Even then, Jake had doubted her reasoning.

"But that'll mean you'll have to go away for training and wind up who knows where. Do you really want that, Ella?"

She'd really wanted that. Allen Terrell had been a career

lawman, starting out with one of the state's field offices then moving on to the FBI in Houston. But he'd retired in his late forties and moved back to the lake for a quieter life and two months later, he and Ella's mother had been killed in that wreck.

Ella took it hard. She'd been close to her daddy. A couple of months later, when the school sponsored a career day, Ella had proclaimed she wanted to follow in her daddy's footsteps. And Jake had foolishly decided that was just a whim.

Ella had been completely serious.

And she'd shown him just how serious.

While he'd gone his way, attending college and working toward becoming a Ranger, she'd gone off to another college then applied for local police work, worked as a patrol officer and then taken the test to become an FBI agent. And she'd passed with flying colors.

That was his Ella.

Actually, she'd never been his Ella.

And, ironically, the very thing that had come between them—her career—was what might help him save Macey now. Why hadn't he seen this back then? Seen Ella's need for justice, the same calling he'd always had in his heart. Had God known this day would come, even when they had no idea?

We were young, too young to even consider getting married.

And he'd thought about having to watch her go out every day to a dangerous job. It was okay for him to do that, of course. But not for the woman he loved.

That point still had thorns in it.

It wasn't meant to be. But he'd gotten married, anyway, maybe just to prove he could carry on without her.

He'd tried. Natalie was a sweet, loving person and she'd given him a beautiful daughter. But he'd often thought about Ella. When he'd been transferred from Houston back to the Garland field office, he'd considered it a blessing. Until his wife found out she had cancer. After Natalie died, Jake brought his daughter back to East Texas. He worked mostly in Tyler now, but Macey had always loved coming to Caddo Lake with her friends. That would change.

If I find her alive.

Now, he was back in this house and his little girl was out there somewhere with a killer. He closed his eyes and tried to pray a midnight prayer but he could only see the bodies of those other girls.

Protect my Macey, Lord.

Jake stomped around the dark house, memories stalking him.

When he heard a noise from the hallway, he whirled around. "Who's there?"

"Me." Ella came into the moonlight, her robe pulled tightly against her body, her arms held just as tightly against the robe. "What are you doing?"

"Watching," he said. "Sorry if I woke you."

"Can't sleep. I miss Zip."

"I guess that dog's trained to watch out for you, huh?"

"Yep. Trained by a friend who's a K-9 officer in Shreveport."

Jake didn't ask if that friend was male or female. If she had a male friend who worked for the Shreveport Police, it wasn't any business of his. Yet, the thought of her with another man made his heart flex. "That's good," he said to ignore his heart. "Maybe we should have kept Zip here."

"And have him go the way of that poor goat?"

Jake turned back from the window. "I guess nothing and no one is really safe right now. I expect reporters to be camped out down on the road in the morning."

"Me, too. I remember…last time."

Jake closed his eyes for a minute. "Yeah, a real circus."

"Do you want some coffee?"

He shook his head. "No. I'm already wired enough."

"I hope the forensic team finds something at one of the drop sites."

"That would help." He ventured closer, his mind twisting with worry for Macey and this new awareness of being near Ella again. He had to focus on his daughter. "I've gone over and over each clue and although I did a thorough search at each site, we both know this man is clever and quick. He sweeps his sites clean."

"Like a team might do," Ella said, her head lifting.

"Yeah." Jake stepped another inch into the kitchen and leaned a shoulder against the arched opening between the kitchen and the living room. "Yeah. His profile suggests he knows the woods, he has some idea of how law enforcement works and he's still young and agile enough to run away." He lifted away from the arch. "He seems to study his victims, too. He knows things and he uses his knowledge in the clues."

Ella grabbed a notepad from the desk by the phone and started writing. "Let's keep a list of anything we might think about or remember. We can compare our notes to what everyone else comes up with and we should pull up the files on the other girls." She jotted down something then glanced back up. "Military, maybe? Or former police officer? Survivalist?"

"Maybe all of the above but survivalist makes sense," Jake replied. "He knows how to get around without making much noise. I think he must wear some kind of special shoes that don't leave legible prints." He ran a hand down his beard stubble. "I'm thinking some sort of moccasins or slippers."

She sank down on a stool and kept writing. After they'd gone back over what they remembered about all the cryptic notes and the other clues, she said, "We need to start thinking like he'd think. And we need all the help we can get."

"The team will increase tomorrow," he replied. "I've had calls from Ranger headquarters with people volunteering to help." He let out a huff of breath.

Ella nodded, her hair sleep-tumbled around her face. "I guess I'll be on the sidelines, but I want to help."

"And I want to keep you safe but I have to find my daughter."

Ella mirrored that with her next words. "I want to find Macey and keep you safe."

Jake stood at the end of the counter, his hands gripping it to keep still. "Who would have thought we'd be back here, trying to find the same man."

"Maybe *he* did," she said, jotting that down. "Maybe he started planning this right after he got away."

Jake steeled himself against the odds. Right now, they were not in his favor. "I'll regret that till my dying day."

Ella stood and moved close, so close he could see the freckles sprinkled like cinnamon across her nose and smell the sweet scent of her shampoo. "I never imagined this nightmare could start back up."

"Me, either." He stared out the window, wondering where Macey was tonight. "I hope she's warm and…not too scared. It gets cold out there these nights."

Ella's eyes held his and then she rushed into his arms. "Jake, I'm so sorry. I wish I could fix this. If I could exchange myself for Macey, I'd do it in a heartbeat."

He held her there, the memory of her in his arms covering him with a familiar warmth while the horror of her words hit him square in the gut. "You can't do that, but having you with me helps. You're one of the best."

She lifted her head, her eyes going a dark-sky blue. "I used to be one of the best. Now I'm not so sure. I'm rusty."

"But you're still the best, Ella. I was so stupid way back long ago."

She patted his shoulder in a way that should comfort him, but it didn't. "It's over now. We both had to do what we needed to do, Jake. And maybe God allowed us to go through losing each other to bring us back to this moment, so I can help you find Macey."

Jake touched a finger to a trailing curl of her honey-brown hair. "Together, side by side."

"Side by side," she replied, the longing in her eyes covering a multitude of wants.

He smiled and for the first time in twenty-four hours, it was a real smile. "That's the plan."

No one was smiling at dawn.

The press had set up shop down at the gate, making it hard for the officials involved in the case to get inside the farm. Sheriff Steward placed an armed deputy at the entrance to keep the reporters and photographers away from the main house.

Jake paced back and forth in the big open kitchen, a cup of coffee in his hand. "Still no word on Luke, either."

Ella brought him a biscuit with ham. "You need to eat."

He took the plump biscuit and the paper napkin she offered but he didn't eat. "I want to get going. It's been over twenty-four hours. The longer we wait—"

"I know," Ella replied, her own stomach too keyed up for food. "Let's see what the task force has to say about any additional evidence they might have found at each of the drop sites."

He finally bit into the biscuit and chewed with a hesitance that showed he didn't even taste the food. "That nutcase has my child in those woods somewhere, or maybe even on the lake, moving around in a pontoon or a houseboat." He turned in a rush. "I need to talk to Sheriff Steward about that."

"He's on it," Ella replied. "Wait till the meeting." She pointed to the biscuit. "Try to eat. It's gonna be a long day."

Jake stared at her, then looked down at the food. "At least we're being fed well. I guess you're the best at anything you set your mind to."

Ella almost bristled at that pointed remark. Considering the tremendous stress Jake was under, however, she let it slide. But she had to wonder if he still resented her career choice.

Growing and cooking food was a whole different thing from tracking a killer.

Maybe she wasn't very good at either.

But up until now, she'd been content with her gardening and her cooking. She loved setting up intimate dinners for her clients and she loved the camaraderie she'd found with the other workers and her grandparents. Growing fresh food, and cooking and serving it on a big, country table had brought her the peace of mind she'd craved for a long time.

But that was all on hold for now. She'd called her employees and told them what she could. A dangerous criminal had kidnapped a young girl and was now hiding out somewhere on the lake. So when her friend had asked, she'd shut things down to help with the search. She warned all of them to be alert and to stay close to home. She prayed they'd listen. She asked God to protect each of her workers. They all had families they loved, too.

And now, Jake was standing here trying to choke down one of her famous biscuits because the solid fear he had in his gut was putting him through the kind of turmoil and angst no father should have to experience.

Two worlds colliding and Ella felt out of control.

So she prayed. And then she checked her rifle.

* * *

"Nothing." Jake paced the same spot he'd been pacing all day. "I should be out there on my own. That's what he wants. That's why he's not making a move today."

Ella's sharp gaze moved over the still woods. "He'll show up sooner or later. He likes the game. He's making us wait since we brought in other people."

"Or he's made his final move and…he'll prove that to us." Jake couldn't stomach that scenario, so he lowered his head and paced some more. "I'm used to working a case. I need something to keep me occupied or I'm gonna go mad, Ella."

The leaves had already turned to shades of red, gold and orange, making the whole forest come alive with fall colors. But each time a leaf floated to earth or a branch twisted in the wind, they all jumped. Jake felt caged here inside this big screened window on the world.

"Let's think," Ella said, guiding him over to where she'd placed her notepad by the big whiteboard they were using to keep track of all the clues in the case. A map of the entire lake hung near the fireplace mantel, with the drop sites marked in red. "Let's talk about old boyfriends or anyone who might have a grudge against Macey."

"Are you kidding me?" he asked, shocked. "You know who this is so why bother? I know it looks suspicious with Luke missing, too, but he's solid. We can rule him out as a suspect."

"We think we know," Ella said, "but what if it's someone else. Someone who's copying the Dead Drop Killer? It's happened before in kidnapping cases."

Jake rubbed his face then shook his head. "He knows things, though. Intimate things. He had your necklace."

"Yes, you found my necklace but someone could have easily found it in the woods somewhere and left it hanging where you found it."

Jake let out a grunt. "Are you trying to distract me or make me go insane?"

She lowered her voice. "I'm trying to come up with every possible scenario, while we're stewing here and doing what seems like nothing, we can...speculate."

Jake had to admit she made some valid points. "But Macey doesn't have any enemies. Everyone loves her. She's been dating Luke for about five months and...they seem happy together." He shrugged. "In spite of being raised by me, she's a pretty sensible kid."

But he had to wonder. What if his daughter had a whole other life? He'd seen it too many times in other young people. He'd brought many of them to justice while their poor naïve parents swore it couldn't be true.

He turned to Ella, his heart sick with a new fear. "If this is a copycat...and let's just say that for a minute...then I need to talk to all of her friends, her teachers and anyone else. Even the place where she works part-time."

"Where is that?" Ella asked.

"A little shop back in Tyler," he said. "She calls it a boutique."

"Let's tell the others and we'll start there," Ella replied. "And we'll work our way to the school and talk to some people there. We can go back to the mall, too. Follow her footsteps, look at surveillance tapes. Anything to help us."

Jake's adrenaline came back in full force. "This is why I came to you— Well, one of the reasons. You still think like an FBI agent."

"I never stopped thinking that way," Ella replied. "Once you've been through this kind of thing—" She stopped, put a hand to her mouth. "Never mind. Let's go."

Jake didn't have to fill in the blanks with what Ella hadn't said. He knew this would scar Macey for life.

If she lived through it.

NINE

After the morning briefing, Ella and Jake headed out to their next destination.

Ella volunteered to drive and now she glanced over at Jake. "So not much new from the crime scene people. But they did find some red-colored fibers on that poor little baby goat."

"That's something at least." Jake sat wedged against the passenger's-side door as if he wanted to bolt at the next stop sign. "I don't know how much more I can take."

Ella's heart did that little twist again. She wanted to take away his pain and his fear, but she didn't have the ability to do that. "Hey, we've got people watching out everywhere. We have the Amber Alert out, too. And we've got a prayer chain going across the state."

"He won't like that."

"Well, tough," she responded, her need to fix this keeping her mind alert. "He should be afraid. Prayer is a powerful thing."

"It didn't save Natalie."

How should Ella respond to that? Thinking about it, she remembered what her granny had told her after her parents had died. "No, God didn't save Natalie in the way we wanted Him to save her, but like Granny used to tell me when I'd get sad about my parents, He did heal her by taking her home."

Jake gave Ella a quick glance. "So if He decides to take Macey home, I should rejoice."

She wasn't doing a very good job of comforting him. "No." She let out a breath. "I don't have any answers except to say that faith will see us through. If the worst happens, it would be horrible and painful and—" She stopped, shook her head. "Let's concentrate on the here and now."

Jake's grunt showed her exactly how much he appreciated her gentle counsel. "Because we can't predict the future and we can't explain why horrible things happen to innocent people."

"Yes, I guess that's about it. The evil of this world seems to win out at times, but God is always in control."

"I wish He'd control this investigation and help us find my daughter. That's my prayer right now."

Ella watched her driving, silent and unsure what to say next.

"Hey?"

She ventured a glance at Jake. "What?"

"I appreciate you trying to make me feel better and… my faith is strong. But…I will always question why God lets something like this happen in the first place. I guess that's human nature."

She couldn't argue with that. "It is, but we have to hold out and do the best we can and remember that He knows we have questions and He knows our hearts."

He tugged his hat down on his head in a manner that seemed to shut her and the world out. "If I find him, I will kill him," he replied. "I'm confessing to that sin ahead of time."

Ella decided she'd have to double her own prayers. Because she felt the same as Jake.

Three hours later, they were again in the truck and headed to talk to the parents of Macey's boyfriend. The principal at the high school had told them the boy hadn't been in school yesterday or today. Ella took a sip of her soft drink and checked on Jake. "You need to eat that hamburger."

Jake stared at the fast food bag on his lap. "I can't seem to choke anything down."

"Try," she suggested. "One bite at a time."

He nibbled the big burger then put it back on the plastic wrap. "I can't sit around and wait, Ella. I need to be out in those woods, searching for Macey."

"We've covered a lot of ground today," she reminded him. "We talked to her teachers, the school staff and we checked where she works part-time. Something might turn up."

Jake wrapped the half-eaten burger and tossed it back in the greasy bag. "And we came up with nothing. No one has seen anybody matching the description of the Dead Drop Killer and no one had anything to offer regarding Macey's actions or whereabouts that afternoon before she was taken."

"Well, we know she attended school and then went to work for two hours," Ella reminded him. "And her friend picked her up from work and they went to the mall."

Jake held a hand on the door handle. "The investigators are gonna go over the mall video footage again, in case we missed anything the other night. I'm hoping they'll find something, anything that will give us a clue."

"We still need to find her boyfriend," Ella reminded him. "It's mighty strange that Luke Hurst hasn't been seen for two days."

"And that he's not returning my calls," Jake replied. "I don't believe he's done anything to Macey, but I am worried."

Ella didn't want to like the boyfriend for this, but she had to go over all the possibilities. What if the boyfriend was copycatting the killer for some reason? Maybe he and Macey had troubles Jake wasn't aware of.

To reassure Jake, Ella said, "Luke has to be upset about this. Maybe he's out looking for Macey, like we first thought."

"But he doesn't know unless her friend told him," Jake said. "I can't reach him and it just hit the news this morning. I should have gone by his parents' house yesterday."

"You were busy trying to find Macey," Ella reminded him. "And you had no way of knowing if she'd seen Luke the night she was taken."

"Exactly." Jake nodded, his expression grim. "I should have called him right away, but I was too busy following the clues. Maybe his parents can shed some light on that." He let out another grunt. "I'm not on my game with this one. We all know to talk to the boyfriend first in these types of cases."

"Look, you found a necklace that looks like one that belonged to me and the last time I was wearing it, I was with a serial killer," Ella replied. "Plus, Macey was taken by someone her friend didn't recognize. That would send anyone into a tailspin." She wanted to add just how much it had rattled her, but Jake already knew that.

He lifted his head up to stare over at her. "You don't need to make excuses for me. It was worse than a tailspin." He studied the road in front of them. "I've never felt anything like this. I mean, there's only been one other time—"

His gaze hit on Ella with a rich golden-brown light. Then he looked away.

Ella swallowed back her fears and checked the GPS on his truck. "We should be at their place in ten minutes."

Jake sank down in the seat and closed his eyes.

Ella hoped he was trying to catch a few winks while she drove the fifteen miles to the Hurst home, but she suspected he was praying. The man sure needed to sleep, but how could he when his child was missing and possibly being held by a dangerous, violent man?

When she turned the big truck into the long driveway to Luke Hurst's house, Jake sat up and blinked. "I must have drifted off."

Ella gave him a worried glance then pulled the truck up to the long, cedar-planked ranch house. "We're here."

Jake got out and stretched his arms in the air, each muscle in his neck and back protesting. "Your couch and I did not get along last night."

"Sorry about that," Ella replied, her eyes full of concern. "You can sleep in the guest bedroom tonight."

"Nah, I'd rather be in the living room. That way I can watch the backyard and the woods."

"Okay."

Glad she wasn't going to argue with him, Jake followed her up to the long, sprawling porch where a string of Christmas lights hung like icicles off the roofline. "I don't know a lot about Luke, but he seems like a good kid. Football player, straight-A student and highly involved in the youth group at our church. He's always been polite around me, but then I tend to terrify the bravest of boyfriends."

Ella let out a little smile before she turned serious. "Let's hope we don't find anything else on him."

Ella knocked and waited, her demeanor calm and professional. But Jake could see fear in her eyes. The same fear that trembled through his system with each passing second.

When the door opened, he didn't know what to expect. But Luke's mother stood there with a surprised look on her face. "Mr. Cavanaugh, I…I just heard on the news—"

Luke's mother motioned them inside, then turned to Ella and introduced herself. "Nadine Hurst." Ella did the same and explained that she was a friend here to help.

Jake nodded, swallowed the lump in his throat. "So you've heard Macey's missing, Mrs. Hurst. And I've heard Luke's missing, too. We went by the high school in Tyler but the office reported him as absent yesterday and today. I can't reach him. Have you heard anything from him?"

The woman started wringing her hands. "I...I don't know where he is. He left for school two days ago but he stays in town with a friend sometimes after work. But he didn't call to check in the other night or last night and I've been calling his phone, leaving messages." She sank down on a chair. "When I heard yesterday that Macey was missing, I got so worried I called the sheriff."

Jake found a seat, his legs going out from under him. Ella sat down on the sofa beside him and across from Luke's mother. "Where's your husband?" Ella asked.

"Out looking for those kids," Mrs. Hurst replied. "We thought maybe they'd run off together but that didn't make any sense. Luke's a senior planning for college and he has work, too." She stopped and stared at Jake. "I told Bert we should check with you, but we didn't realize Macey was missing, too, until..." She stopped, put a hand to her mouth. "What if that man's done something to both of them?"

Jake and Ella sparng into action, calling anyone who might know where Luke could be—former teachers, friends and church members for a start. An APB had already been issued for Luke Hurst. The locals had a description of his vehicle and were currently looking for his truck. Now the media was speculating that Luke might be involved in Macey's disappearance. Jake didn't believe that, but they had to check every angle.

Jake had a bad feeling but it had nothing to do with Luke taking his daughter. "I think our killer has either taken Luke, too, or done something to him."

Ella nodded her agreement while they stood in a corner of the Hurst kitchen. "From all indications, they were happy together. No abuse or violence. Everyone we've called or questioned agreed that can't be the case."

"Which means either Luke got wind that Macey had gone missing or…he stumbled into something and…it cost him his life."

Ella glanced to where Luke's parents sat stone-faced and silent. They'd called Mr. Hurst home and he'd told them he hadn't found any signs of Luke or Macey. She and Jake knew that same feeling. "We have to find Luke," she whispered to Jake. "He might know something or he might be able to lead us to Macey."

Jake turned to face her. "Or he could already be dead."

They'd gone back over Macey's actual kidnapping. "We've questioned her friend Rachel over and over and the girl's story is solid," he said. "The man she describes is taller and thinner than Luke. And besides, if Luke wanted to kidnap Macey, he could just pretend to give her a ride home. This man took her by force."

"It doesn't look good, either way," Ella replied, jotting notes on her phone as she went.

Jake's phone rang, causing both of them to jump to attention. "It's the sheriff," he said, a sinking dread in his stomach.

"Jake, we found Luke Hurst's truck out in the wetlands near the nature preserve. You need to get over here."

"We're on our way." He clicked his phone off and pulled Ella by the arm. Whispering the news in her ear, he headed to Luke's parents.

His mother stood up, her eyes watering. "What is it? Who called?"

Jake took the woman's hand. "They found his truck, but they haven't located Luke yet. We're gonna go check it out." He held tight. "It doesn't mean anything."

"We're going with you," Mr. Hurst said, standing up with his truck keys in his hand.

"No." Ella shook her head. "We'll call if we find him, I promise. But right now, the place is swarming with investigators and law enforcement people. We need you to stay close to home in case Luke tries to call or comes back here."

The couple looked confused and frightened, but finally Mr. Hurst nodded. "Just…call us if—"

"We will," Jake said, his own heart tripling beats. He dreaded going to look at that vehicle, dreaded what they might find. But he had to do his job and…Luke was missing. The truck might give them some more clues.

So he headed to the driver's side. "I'm driving this time."

Ella didn't argue with him. She got in and kept right on typing notes on her smartphone.

"You never forgot how to work a case, did you?" Jake asked, admiring her calm.

"Like riding a bike," she shot back. "I just never dreamed I'd be doing this again and possibly with the same psycho."

"Me, either."

He backed out of the long driveway and then peeled out onto the asphalt, stirring fallen leaves into a whirling frenzy as he pushed the pickup to its limit on the winding Texas road.

They made it around to the other side of the big lake in record time. When Jake pulled his truck up by the swampy area, he saw several Sheriff's Department vehicles surrounding a small white pickup that sat at an odd angle in the shallow water. "That's Luke's truck, all right," he said to Ella.

She stared into the afternoon sunshine. "But where is Luke?"

They got out and hurried toward the crime scene tape, Jake showing his badge, his arm on Ella. "She's with me," he said, his tone daring anyone to say otherwise. Even the two FBI agents who'd been brought in had agreed Ella needed to be in on this one, too.

One of the deputies nodded and explained. "A fisherman found the truck partially submerged in the shallows. The driver's-side door was open." He pointed to an older man sitting on the tailgate of another truck. "The man checked to see if anyone was inside, then he called us. We ran the plates and found out this vehicle belongs to the boy you've been looking for."

Jake took in the scene. "Any sign of a struggle?"

The deputy motioned them forward. "No, no sign of blood anywhere on the vehicle or in the surrounding area, but it could have gotten washed away." He gave a sign to a tow truck. "We were just about to pull the vehicle out and have a closer look when we saw something interesting."

Jake's eyes met Ella's. "Do you think he left a clue here?"

"Let's take a good look."

They waited for the tow truck driver to haul the truck up out of the water. Then the deputy pulled Jake toward the open driver's-side door. He pointed to the sun visor on the driver's side. "We saw this when we went back over the vehicle a second time."

Jake's heart slammed against his chest so hard he had to catch his breath. A pink-and-blue scarf fluttered out from the raised visor like wilted flowers floating over water.

"Macey's scarf. She was wearing that around her neck when I last saw her."

Ella watched as the crime scene techs carefully photographed and bagged the scarf. "So does this mean she was with Luke before she was kidnapped—"

"Or does it mean she was with him at some time last night?" Jake finished.

Ella halted the tech. "Hey, mind if we have a look at that?"

The man nodded but held the scarf in his gloved hands then opened the long twisted material wide. "Nothing but bluebonnets and wildflowers," he said.

But Jake caught a glimpse of something different toward the middle of the delicate material. "Stop." He held up a hand then pointed. "Look, Ella. Something's written there in black ink."

The tech looked down and read the words. "'Sacred scenes unfold.' Shrugging, he stared over at Jake. "What's that supposed t'o mean?"

Ella stepped closer. "It's a verse from the hymn."

Jake put his hands on his hips and lowered his head. "It's also the next clue from the killer."

TEN

"'Sacred scenes unfold.'"

Ella listened as Jake went back over the words scrawled on the floral scarf. They were searching the woods and the swamp for Luke Hurst now, but he couldn't seem to get that scarf out of his mind.

"I wanted to grab her scarf and hold it tight," he said. "It smelled like that lotion she likes to wear. I fussed at her last week about always going by the lotion store in the mall."

Ella stomped over ruts in the earth and pushed on into the sticky marshes of the wetlands located on the west side of the vast lake that had been partially formed from the Great Raft, a logjam on the Red River near what became Shreveport/Bossier in Louisiana.

"Women love those stores," she replied to keep Jake calm. "I haven't been in one in a long time." She looked down at the dry skin and cracked calluses on her hands. Then, because her frustrations were as bubbly and murky as these marshes, she added, "I'm sorry you couldn't keep Macey's scarf."

Jake kicked his boot against a rotting log. "You don't ever want to think of your only daughter's scarf having to go into an evidence bag."

Ella could agree with that statement. "But why was it in Luke's truck? Even if she gave it to Luke, the suspect had to have either stolen it long enough to write on it, or he forced Luke to write that message."

"Or he's got both of them and he's messing with me."

Jake's tone told her he was going to go off the reservation if something didn't break in this case.

"Jake, we've got search parties out all over this area of the marshes," she reminded him. "The dogs are here, too."

Tracking hounds. They could find people, things, or… bodies.

Please, Lord, don't let it be bodies.

The task force had mapped out a grid that would have searchers walking almost arm to arm to cover every square inch of this heavy, swampy thicket. The Sheriff's Department had called in volunteers who'd brought their own trained dogs.

Ella didn't think the Dead Drop Killer would be so bold as to show up here, but then he'd surprised all of them by coming back to life. But would they find another clue, or would they find both Macey and Luke dead?

"His parents must be worried sick," Jake said as he hacked through leafless saplings and decayed stumps. "I hated to call them but I want to be here during the search so I knew they'd want to be nearby, too."

"At least they got by the reporters," Ella replied. "They've been swarming around this place like mad hornets."

"They make things worse."

A hound bellowed off to the left. Jake's head went up and he turned to Ella. "Let's go."

She had no choice but to follow him to the sound of the dog's alert. What had the trained bloodhound found?

"He's alive!"

Jake heard a deputy shouting that phrase to another deputy who had a radio to his mouth.

"Get a bus in here," the one with the radio shouted. "We've found Luke Hurst. He's alive."

Jake pushed his way to the place where a crowd of volunteers and dog handlers had circled a spot underneath a group of cypress knees cropping up like giant mushrooms in green, stagnant water and dirty brown mud.

"What's the situation? Did you find my daughter, too?"

One of the deputies stopped Jake a few feet away. "We found the young man, sir. He has a pulse but it's real weak. Paramedics are en route." Then he shook his head. "No sign of your daughter. I'm sorry."

Jake pushed past the smaller man, a heavy disappointment mixing with a weird relief that told him maybe Macey was still alive somewhere. "Let me see him. His parents are waiting up on the road."

The crowd parted so Jake could get through. And then he saw Luke lying there against the knotty roots and tangled vines, a bloodstain caked like dark red clay against his right temple.

"We checked his vitals," another deputy explained. "A weak, jumpy pulse. No broken bones that I can tell." He glanced toward the road. "He's close to hypothermia. We're gonna move him onto a dry blanket and wrap him up."

"How long has he been exposed?" Jake asked, his heart cracking with each dark thought crashing inside his head.

The young lawman looked helpless. "Hard to say right now. It was chilly the last two nights but not below freezing. Good thing he was wearing a down jacket at least. We'll get a blanket on him, sir, and the ambulance is on its way."

Jake heard the sirens and wondered if the suspect was hiding somewhere watching. Did he think this was cute or funny or clever? Jake held his hands in two tight-fisted vises. He wanted to hit something or somebody.

Then he felt a gentle hand on his arm. "Jake, I'll stay with him until they get here."

Ella.

The warmth of her eyes held him, helped to calm him. He nodded, pushed away the dark thoughts. "I'm gonna call his parents and let them know to meet us at the hospital."

She nodded then moved through the cluster of helpers and onlookers until she was standing near the dirty, coffee-colored mud. After whispering to one of the law officers ministering to Luke, she leaned down low and took one of Luke's hands, then carefully pulled the warming blanket tight around his neck.

Jake didn't stay to see what she was telling the unconscious boy. If he knew Ella, she was telling Luke he'd be okay and that he was safe now. And she was probably saying a prayer to back that up.

"He's stable but still unconscious. He suffered a concussion and possible subarachnoid bleed."

"What does that mean?" Bert Hurst asked.

The doctor touched his own head. "It means edema could set in—swelling that puts pressure on his brain. If that happens, we have to go in and find a way to relieve the pressure."

"Surgery," Nadine said, her eyes watering.

"Yes, ma'am," the doctor replied.

"What are the complications?" Nadine asked, her words choked with emotion.

The doctor gave Luke's parents an understanding stare. "As with any surgery, there are of course complications, Mrs. Hurst. But let's not worry about that right now."

Jake stood off to the side with Ella, listening while the E.R. doctor went on in his professional, monotone voice and tried to reassure Luke's tired, worried parents that their son should wake up soon. But they were watching his brain for signs of bleeding and swelling, which meant he wasn't out of the woods yet.

"We need to question him," Jake whispered to Ella after the doctor left. "He has to wake up." Not only for that, but because Luke was too young to have to go through this. And because Macey cared about the boy. "It's not like the Dead Drop Killer to leave anyone alive. Something's off, but I'm glad it is. Luke's alive at least."

Ella glanced at the Hursts. "Jake, you can't push this. He's in a coma. His brain is very delicate right now. We need to find another way to figure out this clue."

"I'm not worried about the clue," he retorted, his tone full of a simmering anger. "I'm worried about Macey."

The hurt in Ella's eyes caught at his heart. "I'm sorry," He finally said. "It's just I need—"

"You need answers," she replied. "Let's go downstairs and talk."

"But—"

"Jake, if this were someone else's missing child, what would you be doing?"

"I'd be out there pounding the pavement, searching."

"Okay, that's what we need to do. We can check in on Luke and if he wakes up and the doctors let us question him, then we'll find out what happened. For all we know, he had a wreck and wandered off, disoriented, into the swamp."

"You know this is about more than a wreck."

When several people glanced up at his loud tone, Jake knew he'd gone too far. He looked back at Ella, his heart jerking and kicking. "Get me out of here."

Ella lifted a hand toward Luke's parents. "We've got to get back out there, but we'll call and check every hour."

His dad gave Jake a vacant stare. "Thank you."

Jake wanted to say something, but he could only nod before Ella turned him toward the elevator doors at the other side of the long hallway. "C'mon. Some fresh air will help and then we can find somewhere quiet."

Jake didn't argue. And he didn't offer to drive. He was too numb with anger and pain to care.

She took him to a quiet coffee shop near the medical center. "Sacred scenes unfold," Ella repeated out loud, since the phrase had been looping inside her head over and over. When Jake didn't respond, she leaned forward. "You rest and eat a bite and I'll think this through." Then she pushed a glass of water toward him. "And drink something besides coffee."

"Think out loud so I can hear," he said. Then he bit into the ham sandwich she'd ordered him. "If this is our killer, he's becoming more and more sloppy. I have to figure out why."

"Sacred scenes unfold." Ella thought about all the other clues. "This has to be on the lake somewhere, something. But not another church. That would be too obvious."

Jake chewed with a forced measure, his eyes vacant and red-rimmed. "Outside somewhere. Maybe something noticeable."

"But what kind of scene? A picture? Or a real scene with people moving back and forth, driving by—"

Jake dropped his sandwich. "A mural."

Ella's pulse did a spin. "A mural."

Jake took a long drink of water. "We have murals painted on buildings and fences all over East Texas."

"But he's sticking to the areas around the lake." Ella got out her phone. "I'll pull some up and see what might be nearby."

Jake's eyes grew brighter. Ella wanted to give him hope, but this sicko might just be sending them on a wild-goose chase. She'd tried to study the profile from the old cases, but each time she started reading the notes, she felt sick at her stomach, her memories too vivid. There had to be something in there, something they'd missed. But for now, she'd go with their hunch on this.

"There are six different murals in three different places around the lake," she said, her finger scanning over the images. "Some of them depict the oil strike on Caddo Lake and some of them show the history of the pioneers. One shows the steamboats that used to ply the lake."

Jake was already standing to put on his jacket. "Let's go, before it gets dark. We need to check every one of them."

Ella stared longingly at her own uneaten sandwich, grabbed the cookie that had come with it and got up to follow him.

Two hours later, they'd checked out a depiction of a group of wildcatters striking oil on Caddo Lake in 1911. But they'd gone over every inch of the scene on the old brick building. Nothing stood out.

Same with the pioneer murals in another small town near the lake. After checking two smaller depictions— one of the famous bluebonnet wildflowers that grew in this area and the other showing the city of Jefferson in the steamboat days, they were both near exhaustion.

"We've got a couple of more," Ella said. "An about an hour before the sun sets."

"Let's check all of them."

She nodded to Jake as they got back into his truck. "There's one more near Big Cypress Bayou but the location is kind of out of the way. I don't remember if I've ever seen that one up close."

"Is it on a building?" Jake asked, his voice hoarse and husky.

"On the side of an old barn from what I can tell on the internet." She hit at her phone keys. "I didn't get very far with that one—just the location. Let's see if I can find anything else."

"We need to check that one out."

Ella didn't know whether to be glad or to just go with the dread shifting through her system.

About fifteen minutes later, they pulled up to an old dirt lane toward where the directions said this mural was located. Ella found another link she'd missed earlier so she pulled that one up. "A little more history here, it looks like."

She scanned the link and let out a breath then gave Jake a wide-eyed glance. "I...I think we're onto something."

"Read it to me."

"Painted by a local artist in the early 1990s, this mural depicts a scene of home and hearth and a strong Texas-style faith. The artist, who still remains anonymous to this day, signed this work 'Sacred Scenes.'"

Ella stopped reading, a cold chill moving down her spine. "Jake..."

But he was already out of the truck, his weapon raised as he stalked with a cowboy determination toward the old barn.

Ella opened the door, her heart catching as the brilliant golden sunset sent shimmering shadows of burnished orange across the tranquil picture in front of them.

But what was behind this pastoral scene, she wondered, as she ran to catch up with Jake. And what would they find in this old barn?

ELEVEN

Jake stared up at the fading mural, his head spinning as he searched for more clues. The scene depicted an old farmhouse and the surrounding land with a red barn nearby, complete with a buggy and horses. Dark green water surrounded by cypress trees stood in the background. A white church sat off in the distance.

"The name of this is Sacred Scenes?" he asked, even though he'd heard Ella's description with every fiber of his being. "We need to get inside this barn."

She didn't even try to answer his redundant question. "We don't know who owns it."

"I don't care who owns it." He trained his weapon on the old plank doors around the corner. "I don't think we'll have to break in. One of the doors is already smashed in."

He tried to focus on the here and now and his job. But dark images clouded his concentration. Jake blinked away the fears circling him like vines. Ella came around, her gun out in front of her. "On three?"

Jake nodded. "One, two, three—"

A gust of rough wind hit the old door and pushed it open with a crashing force. Jake held his breath but Ella couldn't hide her startled expression.

"Sorry," she said, obviously mortified that she'd stepped back. "I'm okay."

Jake nodded and slowly made his way inside the barn. It wasn't very big. More like a shed. And so old, a good wind *could* actually knock it over. "Hard to see," he said. "Hey, Texas Ranger. Anyone in here?"

No answer except that mournful wind whining through the rotted spots in the old boards.

"I'll go get a flashlight," Ella said. Then she hurried back to the truck. Jake stayed near the door, watching her and the open barn.

She was back in a moment, the flashlight shining through the late-day shadows. Old, rusty equipment lined the dusty perimeters of the structure and more long-dormant dust kicked up each time their boots hit the dirt floors. After a careful search of every nook and cranny, Jake finally took a breath.

"Nothing."

Ella lifted the light up to the rafters. "No loft or attic space. The roof is caved in enough to keep anyone off it."

Jake stared at the dirt floor. "And no hidden doors that I can tell." He stomped back and forth, his heart half hoping they'd find a door and his soul wishing he could just find Macey alive.

Ella turned to glance over at him. "It's getting dark. Let's check the wall once more. Maybe the flashlight will show us something we didn't see before."

He nodded and coughed away the dirty, cloying air.

Once they came back around the side of the barn, he inhaled the fresh gloaming and then noticed the wide field behind the building. "We need to find out who owns this land. Maybe someone knew the artist who painted this."

Ella went back over the mural. "That looks like the same field." She pointed to a slight valley covered with red-and-gold-colored leafy trees. "I can see water back there where the trees have lost some of their leaves. Could that be Big Cypress Bayou?"

Jake squinted against the golden sky. "It is water. That

makes sense since your description said this was near the bayou."

He glanced back at the mural, trying to match it up with this old, abandoned field. "So this barn could be the barn in the picture."

Ella shined the light on the painted barn. "It could be. This was painted about twenty-two years ago, but the barn could have been red at the time. Or a faded red."

Something about the color red nagged at her consciousness, but Ella figured it had to do with all the Christmas decorations they'd seen on their countryside drives.

Jake went up to one of the gray-faced doors. "Bring me the flashlight." Ella hurried over. "Hold it up to this door."

She did as he asked. "I see traces of old red paint. Not much left, but I think this is the barn in the mural."

"Me, too."

He hurried back to the painting. "So this is a sacred place to the killer?"

Ella stared back up at the mural. "Look. I found the words. Remember the article said the artist signed it with that phrase."

Jake came over to the right corner of the mural. The words *Sacred Scenes* were scrawled in black paint against the building. "An anonymous artist who used the same phrase as our suspect."

Ella held the flashlight on the words. "Jake, the artist could *be* our killer."

Jake did the math in his head to slow the hope surging in his heart. "Early 1990s—that means he would have been around twenty or twenty-one, maybe."

"So now he'd be in his early to mid-forties." Ella's body gave out a tremble that she shook off. "Plenty young enough to jog through the woods."

"It also means he grew up around here and this place has some meaning for him," Jake said. "We need to alert the forensic team." Then he turned to her. "Ella, we might find some DNA here that could match up with his DNA—if we find anything on any of the other clues."

"I'll call the sheriff and the forensic team," Ella said, her fingers already tapping her phone.

Jake kept studying the mural, the last rays of sun now slipping behind the horizon to the west. "We'd better stay here and wait for them," he said after Ella hung up. "And maybe we'll hear something on anything they might have found on the other evidence we've turned in so far."

"I hope so," Ella replied, her silhouette etched in shadows and sunshine. "I sure hope so." Then she stared out into the trees. "And I'd feel better if we could search these woods, too."

A few hours later, Ella wondered if the suspect had led them on another merry chase to nowhere. They'd gone back over the barn and gathered evidence on anything from fingerprints to the wood to the brand of the old equipment left inside. The team had checked the floor several times over for trapdoors.

They'd found nothing.

The volunteers and their hounds had scoured the countryside, moving through thickets of bramble and murky, muddy spots of water and trees. So far, they hadn't discovered anything—not one piece of clothing, not a scent to follow and no sign of any other buildings or structures. The woods sat silent and smug in the moonlight, the fat, dark shadows hulking about as if the very trees were guarding a secret.

"What do we do now?" Jake asked. "That verse about the lamb being a sacrifice keeps running through my head." He stood off to the side with Ella, his gaze sweeping over her in desperation that made her heart break. "What if we're too late, Ella? What will I do?"

Ella stepped close but resisted the urge to pull him into her arms. "Jake, stay strong. He's doing this to punish both of us. You were tracking him and I almost killed him. In his mind, we won and now we have to pay."

"But…I'd gladly give him a chance at me. Why'd he have to take Macey?"

That husky crack in his strong voice tore through Ella like an earthquake moving underground. She couldn't stand to see this gentle giant hurting so much.

Dear Lord, please help me. Help me to be strong for Jake and Macey. Give Jake a new strength and help us find her. Please, Lord.

Her quiet prayer seemed redundant and not nearly as precise as she'd like it to be. But Ella knew the Lord didn't care about the presentation. He would hear their prayers. And if the worst happened, He'd see them through.

"He's an evil man," she said, her hand touching Jake's khaki jacket. "He hit you where it would hurt the most."

Jake put his fingers to his eyes. "I just wish I could know she's okay."

Ella moved an inch closer, but a call from one of the deputies caused her to step away from Jake. When they heard the hounds baying, they looked at each other for a brief moment.

"Hey, Ranger Cavanaugh, I think we found something."

Jake pushed past her, his boots hitting on rock and dirt.

Ella hurried after him to the spot in front of the barn where they had set up lights, maps and equipment. Two deputies rushed out of the woods.

One deputy took off his hat and said, "We found an old rowboat tied up and hidden underneath some bramble, about a half mile down the bayou. One of the cadaver dogs alerted."

Jake took a couple of steps. "Where?"

"Stay here, Cavanaugh," the other one said.

"Why?" Jake whirled, then glanced back at the woods. "Why? Tell me now or I'll go see for myself."

The deputy glanced at Ella. She nodded. Jake needed to hear everything. But the sudden activity all around them told her that whatever they'd found was significant. Law officers were scurrying here and there, radios and phones to their ears. The crime scene team and the other dog handlers went into overdrive.

"What's going on?" she asked.

The young deputy lowered his head. "We found…a female body in the boat."

Jake gulped air, put a hand to his mouth. "Macey's only been missing a couple of days. I have to see if—"

Ella thought he might be sick right there. She rubbed Jake's back. "We don't know yet," she said, hoping against hope that it wasn't Macey.

The deputy motioned to another officer. "We found this in the boat, near the body."

The man brought something out of a brown paper bag, his gloved hands holding it up toward the light.

Ella gasped at the sight of the embroidered fabric purse covered with splashes of mud and dirt. It had to have belonged to a young girl.

"Macey's purse," Jake said, tears rolling down his face. "Macey's purse." He reached out, grabbed Ella's arm.

"We found a note inside." The deputy held up the white paper and read. "'We used to go camping. But we got lost on the way. Who knows—today might be your last day.'"

Jake bent double. "He's killed her. He's killed Macey." He let out a slow, keening wail of anguish that tore at Ella's heart. She bent with him, holding his arm, rubbing his back. "Jake—"

Jake stood and glared at the deputy. "Take me to the scene."

* * *

Ella hurried to keep up with Jake but when they reached the crime scene, things seemed to move in slow motion. The crowd of law enforcement people parted like the Red Sea, all eyes on Jake and Ella now. She ran to take his hand and together they walked toward where a cluster of crime scene techs had gathered near a shallow shoreline.

Ella could see the boat. She closed her eyes and prayed a scattered prayer. *Dear God, please, please help us.*

Jake stopped near the old boat and nodded at one of the men standing guard. The girl's body wasn't covered yet but the darkness made it hard for Ella to see. Someone supplied a flashlight as Jake got down on his knees in the mud.

Ella stood back, her breath caught in a sob. Seeing such a strong, proud man on his knees silently weeping just about did her in for good. The woods went silent out of respect as they all waited for Jake to identify the girl.

He sat there for what seemed like an eternity and then he let out a giant gushing sob. "It's not her. It's not my Macey."

Everyone went into action while Ella pushed toward Jake. By the time she'd reached him, he had collapsed against the old boat, his shoulders still shaking, his pain so raw and heavy that everyone around him gave him the space he needed.

While she held his hand and let him cry.

A few minutes later, Jake's pain turned to rage. He stood and paced, his frown daring anyone to speak to him. Ella let him shake off his anger. She wanted to scream right along with him but she needed to keep him on track. She was good at that, at least.

Jake let out a deep-throated scream of rage. "He talked about going camping. What did that note say?"

Ella repeated the ominous words. "We used to go camping. But we got lost on the way. Who knows—today might be your last day."

Jake let out another grunt. "What, he's making up rhymes now?"

"Jake, think. It's another clue so think about campgrounds and maybe about when they're open or when they closed. Or if you've ever been lost in the woods."

He gave her a disgruntled stare. "This isn't about closing time, Ella. He's going to kill Macey."

"He's taunting us. He left Macey's purse there, probably today when we showed up here. He's watching us but we're getting close. We're close, Jake. So close."

Jake wiped at his eyes and leaned down, his hands on his knees and his head down as if he felt sick to his stomach again. "You're right. He's watching us. Maybe it's time we figure out a new plan. Maybe we should give him a show."

"What are you thinking?"

"He was here, obviously." Jake pointed to the woods. "He was in these woods, so he has some means of getting around." He stood tall and glanced around. "We need to go back and look again for tire tracks that are out of place and footprints that lead into the woods."

"We did that," one of the volunteers said.

"We do it again," Ella retorted. "If we have to go back over every inch of each of the places we've been, then we do it."

No one said a word.

Finally, Ella glanced at Jake, then announced, "We need to get the body out of that boat and get it to the morgue immediately. Then first thing in the morning, those of you on the task force need to meet back at my place and we'll go over everything again. We need to revisit this suspect's past crimes to see if we can find more patterns or habits that might help us."

"Are you speaking for him?" someone shouted and pointed at Jake.

"Yes, she is," Jake said, his look daring anyone to question that. "Anybody got a problem with that?"

Silence again.

Jake nodded and put his hat on. "Let's go," he said. But when he started toward the woods, Ella grabbed him by the arm.

"You need to come with me."

"I want to see the crime scene again," he said, his eyes moving from her face to her hand on his arm.

"Jake, you're exhausted. You need to get some rest. You have a team of experts on this. Let them do the footwork while we try to figure out this next clue."

"I need to get on that, too," he said, the plea in his voice hard-edged and stubborn. When she didn't budge, he added, "You might be my spokesperson on procedure but you can't tell me what to do."

"If you don't rest," Ella said, her own tone firm, "you will collapse on your feet and that won't help your daughter." Ella pushed at her hair and took a calming breath. "I can't tell you what to do but I can tell you that you won't be a bit of good if you have to be taken away in an ambulance."

He shot her a look full of a simmering rage, then he pulled his arm away and stalked to the truck.

Ella gave a nod to the people all around. "I appreciate all of you and I know you're good at your jobs. I think the sheriff will agree we need to finish up here and then get back to this first thing in the morning. We'll get a fresh start tomorrow," she said. "But for now, Ranger Cavanaugh is off-limits. Call *me* with any updates."

When she reached the truck, she sat there in the driver's seat for a couple of moments, staring into the dark woods. And she had to wonder. Had they all lost their way?

TWELVE

"You shouldn't have pulled me off this crime scene," Jake spouted the minute they were on the road.

"I had to," Ella replied, her eyes on the black road. Clouds had moved in, causing the night to go as dark as a gray wool blanket settling against the chill in the air. "You're going in circles. You have to let the others do their job."

"You're not even in law enforcement anymore," he said, hitting a hand against the door handle. "You can't tell me what to do."

Ella slammed on the brakes so hard rocks flew up and hit the body of the big truck. She skidded off the road and shut down the engine. "I understand you're worried and angry, but you came to me, remember?"

Jake stared ahead, his jaw jutting in a stubborn silhouette. "I had to warn you."

"I'm warned. I can go back to my life and leave you to it."

He finally lowered his head. "Then I'd have to worry about you, too."

Ella leaned in toward the steering wheel. "You always did take on the world."

"I just take care of my own."

She didn't dare look at him. "But, Jake, I'm not…your own. You don't have to be responsible for me."

"Yes, I do." He turned to stare over at her.

Ella couldn't see his eyes, but she felt the heat of his gaze slamming against her skin. "Jake, you have to listen to me. I'm so thankful you warned me and asked for my help. But I can go back to my world and you can continue on without me if I'm getting in the way or making you uncomfortable." She inhaled, swallowed what she really wanted to say. "But for Macey's sake, I'm here and I'm willing to stay here."

"It'd be dangerous for you, either way," he finally said, his tone full of fatigue and defeat. "I'm sorry but I have to make sure you're safe, too."

Ella saw in that instant that nothing had really changed between them. He'd argued with her about the dangers of this life before she'd ever broken up with him. He didn't want her in law enforcement because he was so afraid something would happen to her. Yet he was willing to take that chance with himself.

But he'd never stopped to think about how she worried in the same way about him. The difference was that she trusted him to do his job and stay safe. She'd always trusted Jake because he made her feel secure…and loved.

Did he still love her? Could he ever really trust her?

If he did, which she doubted, why couldn't he give her that same kind of trust that she felt with him? She had failed at her job and she'd given it up. Maybe that was proof enough that she was a coward.

"I can take care of myself," she reminded him once again while every fiber in her body pushed at her to hold him tight.

He didn't say anything for a moment or so. Then he ran a hand up and down the leg of his jeans as if he were trying to wipe something away. "But…you quit."

Stunned, Ella sat up to glare at him. "What's that supposed to mean?"

"You gave up the FBI. I thought—"

"You thought I'd turned weak and afraid? That I ran out of courage?" She'd certainly just thought the same about herself.

"No, no. I told you I admire your courage. I thought you realized you didn't want this kind of life." He shook his head. "Do you? Do you want this kind of day over and over? Death, criminals, evil people messing with you as if your very life is some sort of twisted game? Do you still want to be back in this, Ella?"

Ella's breath caught in her chest. She couldn't breathe, couldn't think. "Did you come to me to test me, Jake? To see if I still had what it takes to bring in a criminal?"

He ran a hand over his clipped curls. "I'm not saying any of this in the right way. I've always had trouble getting things right."

Ella opened the truck door and got out to find some fresh air, but the cold wind hummed an eerie whine all around her, reminding her that someone could be watching her through that veil of clouds and trees. Had she ever been safe?

Then she heard the passenger's-side door slam and listened to Jake's boots hitting the pavement. He came around the truck and stood in front of her. "Do you think I'm the kind of person to put you through this just to test you? Do you really consider me that kind of man?"

"I don't know how to consider you right now," she admitted. "You're a worried father and you're hurting because you feel so helpless. That's understandable. But you got me involved so you must think I'm good for something or maybe you came to me just to prove a point. Or maybe because you think I'm the only one who can draw this killer out, I don't know. I'm willing to do that, for you, Jake."

Jake held his hands fisted at his side, his hard-edged expression reminding her of a wall of rock. Hard to reach, hard to handle, but oh so easy to love.

Ella immediately regretted their spat. "Jake…"

He grabbed her and pulled her close, his arms surrounding her in that familiar shield of tenderness. "I'm not good at talking," he whispered.

He showed her what he was good at. He kissed her, his mouth grazing over her lips like a gentle wind, his hands moving over her skin with a touch that left her breathless. Ella returned the kiss, her heart opening with longing and memories and tingling warnings.

When he pulled away and stared down at her, she saw the truth there in his eyes. She saw the need, the fear, the regret and the longing.

"Jake?"

"I know, I know." He pushed away and let out a deep breath. "I can't do this. We can't be here, in this place. I've got to find Macey."

Ella gathered herself back into one piece. "Then I'm going to help you, no matter how mad or hateful or mean you get."

He glared at her, then went soft again. "No matter how much I want to kiss you?"

"That, too," she said. Then she got back into the truck and waited for him.

Jake stalked around and climbed back inside, his demeanor less confrontational now. "I can't stop, Ella. I can't rest."

"Yes, you can," she replied. "You will rest while I take over for you. I won't stop."

"And when will you rest?"

She started the engine and pulled back out onto the

road. "After we find Macey…and get this madman, I'll rest then. Or I'll die trying."

He touched a hand to her cheek. "And that's what scares me the most."

In spite of trying to stay awake, Jake passed out the minute he hit the big cushioned sofa in Ella's living room.

A sound woke him at around three a.m., causing him to sit straight up and go for his gun. Car doors opened and shut and a dog barked low and sure.

Zip?

Jake lowered his pistol and walked in his sock feet to the front window. Sure enough, Ella's grandparents were ambling their way up to the back door. He opened it and turned on the back porch light so they could see to get up the steps.

"Jake, is that you?" Wilson Terrell asked, squinting through his heavy glasses.

"Yes, sir." Jake stepped out to help with suitcases and bags. "Did y'all see the guards posted up on the road?"

"Yep," Wilson replied while Zip scooted by him to sniff at Jake's jeans. "They checked us out before letting us pass." He glanced around the property. "We saw lawmen all over the place."

Jake heard a hint of a disgruntled tone in that comment. "Good. That means they're doing their jobs."

Wilson gave him a quick scowl then allowed his wife to go ahead of him into the house. Zip followed her.

Edna smiled up at Jake. "He got it in his head that we were coming home so we got up and loaded up. Where's Ella?"

"In her room, last I checked."

Out of habit, Jake surveyed the yard and the surrounding buildings. They had officers posted at each one, but he couldn't shake the feeling that they were still in danger.

So when he got back inside, he put out a call on the radio for everyone to check in. All of the officers responded in a prompt manner.

Then Ella walked into the kitchen, her hair all mushed and her fluffy robe cuddling her in the same way Jake wished he could. "Granny."

Her grandmother hugged her close. "Your grandpa woke up and said, 'Let's go home,' so here we are, honey."

Ella let go of her grandmother then sank on the floor to hug Zip. "Zippy." The big burnished dog gave her several happy doggy kisses and woofed a greeting. "I missed you so much," she said, her gaze hitting on Jake before it moved on.

Jake stood to the side, his heart doing a flip-flop kind of wobble as he watched Ella's family reunite. A piercing hurt hit him in the gut. He missed Macey. Missed her with an agonizing pain that made him feel like a crippled, broken man. And he missed this—having family to hug close, to love, to cherish.

Ella glanced back at him. "I'll make coffee."

He helped her up and nodded. "I checked with all the patrols. Everything's okay."

Wilson looked from one to the other. "How you two holding up?"

"It's been tough," Ella admitted as she went about getting together an early morning breakfast. Without giving them too many details, she went over what had happened so far. "So we're trying to put things together to give us a clue as to who this man might be and to figure out where he might be keeping Macey."

Edna glanced at Jake. "We had to come back. We can help out around the house and help feed everyone. Zip can do his job and help guard." She put a hand on Ella's arm. "We'll worry less if we can see you with our own eyes."

"I'm glad you're home," Ella said. "Just be careful and

always do what the law officers tell you. I don't need either of you being heroes, okay?"

"I ain't nobody's hero," her grandfather said on a huff of disgust. "But I will protect what's mine."

"Wilson, do you want to get banished back to Gilmer?" his wife asked.

"No."

Jake had to smile at the scowl on Wilson's wizened face. At least Ella's stubborn grandparents brought a little levity to the situation.

"Did you sleep?" Ella asked while she buttered toast.

He checked his watch then offered a surprised glance. "Yes. Almost three hours or so."

"Good." She didn't say anything else.

Jake did feel refreshed but he'd rather forgo breakfast and get out to the command center to go over all the evidence again. "I think I'll get a shower before I eat," he told her.

"Okay." She handed him a steaming cup of black coffee. "I'll save you some toast and eggs."

He didn't miss the warmth of her eyes moving over him. Was she remembering that kiss they'd shared earlier?

Jake hurried down the long hallway toward the guest bathroom, grabbing some clean clothes and toiletry items a fellow Ranger had brought for him yesterday. After a quick hot-water shower that loosened his tired, sleepy joints, he was soon right back in the kitchen asking for more coffee.

And he was right back into worrying about his daughter.

Ella glanced up when he entered the room, her eyes widening. "Wow, you sure clean up nicely, Ranger Cavanaugh."

Jake enjoyed the warm invitation he saw in her expression. Enjoyed it and promised himself he'd remember it later.

Much later. After his Macey was safe at home again.

He had no business feeling these feelings toward Ella right in the middle of trying to save his daughter from a serial killer. What kind of father was he, anyway?

The kind who needed someone like Ella in his life, he told himself. The kind who'd do everything in his power to protect those he held dear. Including Ella Terrell.

Ella held up a plate of eggs, grits and toast. "Told you I'd save you some breakfast."

Jake reached for a piece of toast, his gaze locking with hers, when Zip went into a tailspin and started barking a hostile rant. The big dog's paws tapped an urgent warning against the floor and then, still barking in rapid-fire cadence, Zip lurched toward the side window and snarled a warning that someone he didn't like was approaching the house.

THIRTEEN

Jake and Ella both went for their firearms. Ella called out to Zip and calmed the dog. Her grandfather coaxed Zip away from the window, then grabbed his shotgun. But before Jake could get out the door, they heard voices and then a shout.

"Stop right there!"

Jake listened, his gun drawn. "It's one of our men," he said in answer to the shouted command.

He headed out the back door, Ella right behind him.

Seeing two deputies with drawn guns, Jake turned toward the bushes and let out a sigh. "A reporter."

A sheepish-looking man with several cameras strapped around his neck stared at the deputies with big, frightened eyes, his hands up in the air. "I'm sorry. Just wanted a closer look inside."

"Why?" Ella called out, anger in the one word.

The man whipped his head around to glint at her. "You've been hiding out here in plain sight, Ms. Terrell. We just want a few comments about how you feel regarding the return of the Dead Drop Killer. And why you're so involved in this case."

Jake gave one of the deputies a glance. The deputy stepped forward. "You're trespassing, Mister. I'm gonna let you off with a warning this time." He tugged the man out of the bushes and slung him toward Jake. "But next time, I'll have to turn you over to this Texas Ranger. You won't like that, I can assure you."

Jake stepped in front of the scared photographer and lifted the man by his coat lapels. "One warning, understand? We have no comments at this time, so don't come back up here looking for anything. We'll release a statement when we have more facts."

The man might be scared, but he was determined. "But aren't you putting people in danger by keeping this under wraps? What about the upcoming Christmas Festival later this week?"

"What about it?" Jake asked, his head spinning with all the scenarios a large crowd of people could bring.

"Don't you think it's dangerous to go on with the festival even though a possible killer is on the loose?" He leaned in toward Jake. "Especially when your own daughter is still missing?"

Jake lifted the man off the ground and put his nose in the photographer's face. "You need to get off this property, right now."

One of the deputies eased the man out of Jake's viselike grip. "We'll escort him back to the road," he said. "And we'll do a thorough background check on him."

The little man shot a glance back at Ella and Jake. "The public deserves to know what's going on," he shouted. "The local town council says the festival will go on, no matter what. You need to consider that, don't you?"

After the commotion died down, one of the deputies turned back to Jake. "He does have a point. The sheriff is concerned about the big festival this weekend. It's put on by several towns and brings in all kinds of people from all over East Texas." He glanced toward Ella. "Aren't you usually involved in that?"

Ella nodded. "I was scheduled to give tours of the whole

farm and serve hot chocolate and Christmas cookies. I called the people on the committee and told them I had an emergency and I might not be able to open for tours, but I have no control over them calling off the whole festival."

Jake raked a hand down his face. "Just one more thing to consider in all of this. Let's get the task force together and maybe the sheriff can prepare a statement. I think everyone is aware of what's going on, but we don't need any hotheads taking the law into their own hands."

The young deputy nodded. "We've already gotten some tips that turned out to be nothing at all."

Jake's head went up. "Such as?"

"Psychics saying they know where the killer is hiding. People who claim they've seen Macey." He held up a hand. "We've checked into all of them, Ranger Cavanaugh. Nothing has panned out."

Jake pinched two fingers against his nose. He couldn't be everywhere at once. He had to trust in the Lord and these officers who were doing their best to help him. "Okay. What else?"

"Some of the lab reports have come back, too. We'll hear more at this morning's briefing."

Jake and Ella both nodded. "We'll be down to the restaurant kitchen soon," Ella replied.

They went back inside, but Jake had lost his appetite. He stared at the congealed grits and eggs on his plate. "I'm gonna get on out there and look around," he finally said. Then he grabbed his jacket from the back of a chair and took off.

Ella turned to her grandmother. "I don't know what to do for him, Granny."

Edna took Ella into her arms and rubbed her back. "That's why we're here, honey. You can't solve this all alone and you can't put yourself in this kind of danger again. You lean on us. We'll be here and we'll be alert."

Ella prayed so. "I am glad to see y'all."

Zip came to nudge at her leg. "And you, too, fellow."

A few minutes later, she'd had a shower and was dressed for the chilly morning in jeans, boots and a fleece jacket with matching hat. They had a lot to discuss down at the command center.

"Should we prepare sandwiches for lunch?" Granny asked, already rummaging through the refrigerator.

"Yes, but I'll help." Ella went about grabbing her rucksack and other supplies, including her gun.

"I can call one of the other workers," her granddaddy said. "They've all been calling us, anyway. Might do 'em good to help out."

"Okay. Just be careful. And make sure they check in and sign the volunteer sheet. I'll pay them for their time but everyone has to sign the daily check-in sheet." Ella hugged each of them and called to Zip. "Wanna go for a walk, boy?"

The big dog woofed a definite yes and hurried after her.

"I'll let y'all know if we leave the premises," she said.

Her grandparents stared after her, reminding Ella of all the times she'd left with them standing at the door waving to her and telling her to be safe.

Would she ever feel truly safe again?

I know You are watching over all of us, Lord. But I need You to help me resist temptation right now. Help me to focus on finding Macey and help me to do my job so we can catch this person.

Ella had to keep on the task ahead.

Because last night, in Jake's arms, she'd finally felt safe again, at least for those few precious moments. But Ella couldn't count on that feeling. She'd taken the safety of Jake's arms for granted when they were young and in love. Then when he'd offered her those same arms again after her ordeal with the Dead Drop Killer, she'd wanted to stay with him forever. But too many obstacles had still stood in their way. He'd just lost his wife. And Ella had considered herself damaged and too afraid to get close to anyone. Especially Jake. She still felt that way, but his kiss had knocked down some of her defenses.

I pushed him away. I can do it again. I have to do it again. He's too caught up in this case right now to think straight. I won't take advantage of that.

And she wouldn't let down her guard, either.

They both had too much at stake this time.

"What little bit of blood we found on the daisy necklace belonged to you, Miss Terrell," Sheriff Steward explained. "No trace of any fingerprints or anything else to go by there." He gave her a sympathetic glance then continued. "We did discover one possible connection. The same red fibers we found on the little goat were also found on the unidentified body in the rowboat. The techs can't be completely sure, but they're confident those fibers came from the same material."

Ella nodded at the robust sheriff, memories of her necklace being yanked off her causing her to touch a hand to her neck. But that red fiber stuff made her wish she could figure out what was hiding in her memories.

The sheriff went on. "And we've gone back to the playground and the park where y'all talked to the female jogger. We didn't find anything on any of the equipment or along the path through the woods."

"Did you question Mrs. Parsons again?" Ella asked.

One of the deputies nodded. "She told us the same thing she told y'all. He ran by her and pushed her off the path." He shrugged. "She couldn't remember anything much, but she did give a description—the same one we've used on all the BOLOs and Amber Alerts. Tall and slender, dressed in black with the hoodie pulled down over his face."

"The same description I remember from all those years ago," Ella replied. "I never saw his face." She put a hand to her hair. "He...he wouldn't let me look at him."

"Maybe he's ashamed of what he's done," someone suggested.

"Or maybe he just doesn't want to be identified," Jake retorted. "What about the blood we found on Macey's sweater?"

The sheriff shuffled his feet. "It was Macey's blood, Jake. But that doesn't mean she's hurt or anything."

"It sounds like she's bleeding," Jake said on a low growl. "Or worse."

"Or he could have done something to make sure her blood showed up on the sweater."

Jake closed his eyes tightly together.

Ella put a hand on his arm. "We've got people searching all over these woods, Jake."

His eyes snapped open. "I hope they're not too late. He told me I'd regret bringing people in. And he's right. I do."

One of the other Rangers stepped forward. "Jake, man, you know how this works. No one, not even you, can handle something like this alone. Not when it involves a family member."

"Go on," Ella said, encouraging the sheriff to continue.

The sheriff nodded. "So the red fibers...we do know the fibers contain wool and polyester. The techs narrowed it down to certain materials, probably a jacket or sweater purchased from a big outdoors store or a discount store. But the fibers are old and faded, probably from the elements."

"That really helps," Jake said in disgust. "Like I have time to check every store in the area for red fibers."

"I've got people on that," the sheriff replied on a calm note. "If the techs can keep matching those fibers to anything else we find, maybe we'll come up with some sort of garment to match."

"It's something," Ella replied. "If we can narrow down where the item of clothing might have been purchased, we might be able to view video from the store."

Jake leaned his knuckles on the table, his eyes on the vast map of Caddo Lake and the surrounding towns. "I don't have the luxury to wait around for those results."

"Any solid leads on the shoe prints?" Ella asked.

"Still working on that one, according to the crime scene team. Definitely light-footed and, as you said, almost like slippers. But it has to be some sort of fancy running shoe since he gets away so quickly."

"We should check with any local running clubs," someone suggested. "Or check with people who jog along the lake a lot."

Everyone took notes and volunteered for the assignments. Ella thought about asking Mrs. Parsons if she'd noticed anyone wearing red or wearing distinctive running shoes.

The sheriff looked back at Jake. "You could dig a little deeper on the mural, Jake," the sheriff said. "We're waiting on the medical examiner's report regarding the body we found and we're doing a search of any missing women in this area in the last few months. Once we connect on the victim's name, we might have something more to go on."

Jake raised himself up and stood tall now. "The mural. Maybe that's the key. The body was obviously put in that boat to throw us off, but if this man was a local artist in the '90s, maybe we can find him through the local art organizations."

"We'll get right on that," Ella said, glad for something to focus on besides her need to hold Jake tight and never let him go. But after they'd found the body last night, the focus had turned to that. Maybe she and Jake could revisit the mural and go over it with a clear eye in the light of day. Something was nagging at her, but she couldn't remember what. Maybe the mural would jog her memories loose.

Sheriff Steward stepped around the table. "I'll take care of the press conference. Don't have much to offer but I'll try to calm everyone down and assure them we're on this 24/7." He slapped Jake on the back. "Don't give up, son. We're gonna find your daughter."

Jake shook his hand and thanked him. "Thank you, Sheriff. I hope so."

Ella waited for the sheriff to give orders to the task force then followed Jake out to his truck. "We need to check on Luke, too."

"I'm gonna call his parents, but since they haven't called us, I'm thinking he's still in a coma."

"Yes, me, too." Ella took the keys he offered her and got into the big truck. "I know what you're thinking. Today will be the third day since he took Macey."

Jake adjusted his hat and pivoted on the seat. "And we know what each tomorrow means. The fourth or fifth day, Ella. We always found the others on the fourth day or fifth day."

"We've got a few days at least, Jake. And I intend to use every hour of those days to figure this out."

He gave her a look that tore through her resistance. "I couldn't make it without you. You know that, don't you?"

"I do," she said, her eyes holding his. "I do. I'm not going anywhere. Ever again."

He held her there, his lion-like eyes turning gentle and still. "I'll remember that, you know."

"I hope so," she said, wondering why she was walking back into dangerous territory. But then, she'd walk through fire for this particular man. And from the look of things regarding this case and this killer, that's exactly what she'd have to do.

FOURTEEN

"This place looks so peaceful in the morning light."

Jake scanned the old barn and the surrounding woods, his mind trying to absorb the evil that darkened the shadows and hid from the sun's unyielding spotlight. Was his little girl out there somewhere, cold and scared?

He lowered his head, that image tearing at his gut like a jagged knife.

Beside him, Ella stomped her booted feet and blew on her hands. "Chilly this morning. Soon it'll be Christmas."

Jake turned to take in the sight of her so he could wash the darkness out of his soul. She looked so young and cute in her fleece hat, her golden-brown hair scattered around her jacket collar like fallen leaves, her mouth as pretty and enticing as the first time he'd kissed her.

Which only made him remember how he'd kissed her last night. Christmas was approaching and he wanted his daughter home with him to celebrate. He'd even set foot back in a church and attend the Christmas Eve service with Macey.

Ella turned and gave him a penetrating stare. "Jake?"

Jake shook off the need to kiss her again and told himself to get back on track. He couldn't fall in love with Ella all over again in the middle of trying to find Macey. He had to ask again. What kind of man would do that?

The kind who needed a good woman in his life.

No. Not now. Maybe not ever, after this.

If anything happened to Macey…

"Jake?"

"I'm okay," he said to the panic in her question. "I'm okay. Let's get to it."

He stalked away toward the old barn, his heart reminding him that he wasn't the kind of man to be rude to a woman on purpose. But his head didn't care who he mowed over in order to save his daughter. He'd have to be careful handling Ella. She always did pick up on his moods.

He heard Ella traipsing behind him, heard the silence that settled over them with all the heat of the rising sun. But he kept his eyes on the mural and took in the hues and tones of the faded wood. He looked up at the old painting then looked out over the woods.

"So we think this scene depicts these woods and this place," he said in a low, professional-grade tone. He pointed to the church and the house painted off at a distance from the old barn. When he gazed into the open pasture near the water, he didn't see a house in real life. "What happened to the house, I wonder."

"We can take a walk down into the pasture," Ella suggested, her tone blank and as faded as the paint on this old wall.

"Okay, but let's make sure we're not missing anything first."

She nodded, put on her sunglasses. "This must have been a pretty mural when it was first done."

Jake focused on the faded colors in front of him. "Yep."

"So if he painted this when he was younger and then he started kidnapping girls later, he would have started in his mid-twenties and he'd have been in his thirties about five years ago—when he took the last girl and then me."

Jake listened, analyzed and stayed professional. "Yep."

"So he could be over forty by now, if he survived."

"I guess so."

"Jake?"

Jake turned to find a flash of fire in Ella's expression. "What?"

"I know you're a man of few words, but are you angry at me this morning?"

"No." He studied the angle of the house and the church in the mural. The house was more to the east of the woods but closer to the water. The church seemed familiar yet... almost out of place.

"What is your problem?" Ella finally asked.

And he finally turned to face her. "My problem? My daughter is missing...and you're back in my life."

Jake bit his lip, wishing he could take back those words.

Shock colored Ella's face a pretty pink. "I'm sorry. I told you I could walk away, let you and the rest take over. You don't really need me."

He gave her an agonized stare. "I do need you and that's part of the problem."

"So if I stay, I'm a distraction? But if I go, I'm still a distraction?"

He whirled around, unable to filter the words. "You've been a distraction to me for most of my life."

Ella's face seemed to fall right there in front of him. Her eyes, usually so vibrant, went hollow and her expression went from questioning to resigned. "I didn't realize how much you still resent me."

Jake stalked close. "I don't resent you. After I found that necklace, I knew I had to get to you and make sure you were safe. But—"

"But you also wanted to rush out and find Macey."

"Yes." He nodded, let out a breath. "It was like being caught in a vise, having to alert you while I needed to be out there searching for her."

Ella's expression changed to a wall of understanding. "And he knew that, Jake. He knew exactly what that choice would do to you."

Jake lowered his head and stared down at his scuffed boots. "I've been taking it out on you, even while I'm trying to protect you."

Ella touched his arm. "I understand. I can't imagine—"

"You don't have to imagine. You've been there."

She tilted her head, her gaze moving over the building. "Yes, I've been there. Each clue and every article he's left for us only makes me think of things I've tried so hard to forget."

Feeling like a regular jerk, Jake put his hands in his jacket pockets and gave her a long glance. "You never did talk about it. Want to now?"

She shrugged but it looked a lot like a shudder. "Not much to tell. He kept me blindfolded a lot, with my hands tied during the day so we could move through the woods. He moved me from place to place and at night…he'd tie my feet, too."

She looked down at the ground. "He did other things to me at night."

Jake's heart shattered into a million pieces. "What are you saying, Ella? What did he do to you?"

"That's the part I've never wanted to tell anyone," she said, her eyes blank and distant. "You don't need to hear the details now, either."

Too late. Jake moved toward her but she stepped back. That one movement stopped him on the spot. "Is…is that why you pushed me away after we found you?"

She nodded, looked out into the woods. "I didn't want anyone to know so I begged the authorities to keep it quiet."

Jake thought back over all the reports. He hadn't seen her official statement but he'd heard the general details.

He'd been so glad to have her back, he hadn't cared about the rest.

"But that's not in any of the reports on the other girls. Did he—"

"He didn't touch any of them in that way. He saved himself for me," she said. "He told me that right before… he assaulted me." She shrugged. "At the time, I thought he assaulted me because he was so angry that I'd come after him. Now I think it must have been about much more than that."

She couldn't even say the word. Jake turned away from her and leaned one hand on the old barn, nausea making him weak, anger making him strong. "I'm so sorry. You should have told me."

He saw a movement and looked up to find her wiping her eyes. "How could I? I couldn't let you feel sorry for me or think you had to make me whole again."

Jake gritted his teeth at the implications of that statement. "I could have helped you through. You have to know I would have stood by you, no matter what."

"Exactly," she said on a tone of regret.

Jake didn't know how many more harsh surprises he could take. "All this time, I thought you just didn't want me in your life ever again. That you'd chosen the FBI over me. Over us."

She lifted her head and pinned him with her famous Ella gaze. "And all this time, I thought I shouldn't have to make a choice between the two. And that you shouldn't have to make a decision that you'd regret. I had to let you go, Jake."

"Let me go?" He stalked close, then shook his head. "You told me to leave."

"Yes, I did."

She looked so crestfallen. He couldn't believe it had been easy for her. She'd believed he'd think less of her, but she had been so wrong on that.

"You needed me too much?"

"I needed you more than you'll ever know."

"But—"

"But your little girl needed you more."

Jake could see it all so clearly now. How many more sacrifices would Ella be willing to make for his sake? How long would she put herself at risk to catch this killer?

He knew the answer to that. She'd want to save Macey, for him. No matter what.

Jake was about to tell her that she couldn't keep doing things like that but the look in her eyes stopped him. He followed her gaze. "What is it?"

Ella stood staring up at the mural. "The church." She stepped back and took in the whole big picture. "Jake, that's my church. That's where I sang the solo. We've remodeled and updated since then, but that's Caddo Chapel Church."

Jake squinted up at the mural. "And that's why it seemed so familiar…and out of place."

Ella paced in front of the mural. "Sacred scenes unfold." She pointed to the church. "My church." Then she lifted a hand to the faded blue water. "The lake." Next, she raced to the spot where the old house was painted in. "Echoes of the past, maybe?"

Jake was listening and he was beginning to see what she'd realized. "The mother and father with a child—father, mother, praying?"

Ella nodded. "He's left most of the clues right here. But he painted this over twenty years ago."

Jake studied the mural again. "Which means he knew where your church was even at a young age."

"He knew about the church. Maybe his family attended for a long time."

"And maybe he knew you when you were very young."

She nodded. "And even later when I got older."

"He's known you all of your life."

"We don't know that but, yes, it could be."

"So why go after the other girls?"

Ella pushed at her hat. "They were all young—no older than fifteen or sixteen. That's how old I was when I sang the solo at church."

Jake stomped around then gave her another long stare. "And, they all kind of favored you, too."

Ella's eyebrows shot up. "You know, you're right about that. I never considered that he was comparing them to me when I was *younger*. I didn't notice the connection." She took off her hat and shoved it into her jacket pocket. "And I never considered that he was after me all the time."

"Then why did he take Macey?"

She pushed at her hair and kicked one booted foot at the dirt. "To draw both of us out, of course."

"We figured that already, but this makes it even more sinister and intense." Jake reached over to push at her wayward bangs. "He's not done with us, Ella."

"No, he's not."

"And I'm sure not done with him."

A chill seemed to settle over the morning as a dark cloud covered the sun.

Ella's eye met Jake's and held him there. "I won't go down without a fight, Jake. And I won't let him hurt me the way he did before. And if he's hurt Macey—"

"You won't have to worry about that, honey. I'll kill him before I let him lay a hand on you or her ever again."

Then he took her into his arms and held her there near the old, faded mural.

Ella fell against him and wrapped her arms around his neck. "He seems to think I'm sacred, that I'm part of his precious memories and sacred scenes. I'm not, however."

"You're sacred to me," Jake replied, meaning it.

"I'm not a saint, Jake," she mumbled. "I'm just a woman

who wants to finally be free of all of this." Then she burrowed closer. "And I want Macey free of all of this, too."

Jake reluctantly moved away and stared down at her. "Then we'd better get back to work." He glanced up at the barn. "We need to go back over your church records, look at pictures. Maybe you'll recognize someone or see something that will trigger a memory."

She nodded in agreement. "And we need to find pictures of this house. If we can find the house, we might at least find someone who remembers him."

He felt Ella's shudder and he saw the fear in her eyes. Followed by a solid resolve. "If we ever find him, I'll make sure he never forgets *us*. I can promise you that."

Jake's phone buzzed, causing them to break apart.

"Ranger Cavanaugh?"

Luke's father.

"Just wanted you to know Luke woke up this morning. He's still slipping in and out of consciousness but the doctors think he'll be okay."

"That's good news," Jake said. "Glad to hear it."

Before he could ask to come by and question Luke, Bert Hurst spoke again. "He's been asking for Macey. And you. He seems to want to tell you something urgent. I promised him I'd find you."

"I'm on my way," Jake replied. He put away his phone and turned to Ella. "Luke wants to talk to me."

"Let's go," Ella said, rushing toward the truck.

Jake hopped into the driver's side and waited for her to hand him the keys. "We might have a couple of breaks at last."

FIFTEEN

Ella tried to watch the speedometer but finally gave up. Jake was driving to beat the band and she didn't have the nerve to tell him to slow down.

"Heavy traffic!" he exclaimed with a slap on the steering wheel, his frustrated frown aimed at the big truck moving slowly in front of them. "On back roads. Seriously?"

Now she was worried. When he tried to pass the truck and couldn't because of oncoming traffic, she said, "Don't have a wreck trying to get back to the hospital. That won't help anyone."

"Nothing I'm doing is helping," he replied with another pounding on the wheel. But he did pull back a distance from the lumbering truck.

Ella let out the breath she'd been holding. She was beginning to see that his steering wheel took a lot of abuse. She'd seen him do this several times now and, actually, she'd hit at the wheel a couple times herself.

"You're doing everything humanly possible," she reminded him. "We all are."

That statement grounded him. "I should be thankful for the help and I am. I just need some action, something to give us hope."

"Maybe Luke can shed some light on things. He obviously needs to talk to you. He might be able to give us a solid lead."

Jake's curt nod silenced Ella. She wasn't telling him anything he didn't already know. He wanted action, so she took out her phone and pulled up the photos she'd snapped of the mural.

"So once we've talked to Luke, and depending on what he tells us, I'll go by the church office and ask to see old directories. We update them every few years with headshots of members and their addresses but the church historian keeps a copy of each one. Hopefully, I'll be able to find something or maybe seeing someone will jog my memory."

"That sounds like the next logical step," he said, his eyes on the road. "The sheriff promised an update every few hours, too."

Ella scrolled through the pictures of the mural. "I need to call the head of the festival committee and get an update on that."

"Tell me about the festival," Jake said. "Where is this thing held?"

"Various places, but the main event is in the big state park. It's on the lake, of course, but they make a ton of money off the gate fees. We set up tents for vendors—mostly local organizations trying to raise money for their various causes—and artists selling their wares. It's a big deal, economically. Brings in a lot of people from all over the Ark-La-Tex. I usually hold tours and give lectures on growing and buying whole foods and eating organically."

"But you canceled all activity on the farm, right?"

"Yes." She closed out the mural photos and tapped on her email icon. "I have several unread emails from various committee people, probably wanting to know why I'm canceling. They can't see past the moneymaker this festival has become, but I'll try to explain."

"You don't owe anyone an explanation. You can't risk your life or anyone else's."

She had to smile at the conviction in that statement. No, she didn't have to explain her actions to anyone else, but she did owe *him* a lot. Jake might have let her go when they were young and naive, but he'd come to her aid through the years and he'd been right there with her during the worst of her life. He'd come to her now, to protect her and to ask for her help with this situation. Ella didn't know which way to go now, with him always around…and with that kiss lingering between them like lake mist.

Did he keep coming back to remind her of what she'd lost?

Or maybe to show her what she'd left behind?

Right now, he'd come here to save his daughter and Ella needed to remember that.

Jake's phone rang again. He tossed it to Ella. "I need to focus on getting to the hospital."

Ella stared at it then saw the caller ID. "It's the sheriff. Maybe he has a new update."

Jake's eyebrows went up. "See what he has to report."

Ella answered. "Hello, Sheriff Steward. Jake's driving. We got a call from Luke Hurst's father—"

"I know," the sheriff replied on a rush of breath. "We got a situation here, Miss Terrell. Someone tried to tamper with Luke Hurst's medical equipment. Happened right after his father started calling everyone to let them know he'd woken up."

Her eyes cut to Jake. "Is…is Luke okay?"

"He's fine. He had his eyes closed, but he was conscious so he had enough time to see them and hit the alert button."

"Where was the guard we put on his door?"

"We don't know. Can't find him and he's not responding to our radio or cell calls."

Jake had already floored it, but she felt the need to let the sheriff know. "We're almost there."

She ended the conversation and stared over at Jake. "I guess you heard most of that. Someone was in Luke's room, tampering with the medical equipment, but he was awake and alerted the nurses. He was able to hit his call button."

Jake's grim expression summed things up. "So somebody wants to keep Luke quiet—permanently."

She nodded. "Luke needs to tell us something and whoever was in his room doesn't want that to happen."

Jake turned into the hospital parking lot on two wheels. "We'll have to be even more diligent in keeping Luke alive."

"One more person to add to our protection list," Ella replied. "I hope we can find whoever was in that room."

"I can't be sure, but I think it was the same person I saw with Macey the other night."

Jake and Ella listened while Luke struggled with each word. He was pale and scared and still confused. But the frantic brightness in his eyes told Jake that the boy knew something important. And Luke's confusion and explanation also told them that he'd had nothing to do with Macey's disappearance.

"What happened that night?" Ella asked on a gentle coaxing. "Did you see Macey with someone?"

Luke rolled his head as if that action might jar some memories. "Was gonna give her a ride home." He stopped, swallowed and closed his eyes. When he opened them again, his expression held a stark clarity. "Truck swerving out of the parking lot… Thought I saw Macey inside. So I followed…. I got close enough… Macey? Wasn't there."

Disappointment drained through Jake's system. "You didn't see her?"

Luke drifted away.

"Luke? Luke, what about Macey?" Jake ground out the words.

The boy opened his eyes. "Think I saw her again but he pushed her…down. Looked so scared. Terrified. Followed."

"Where did they go?" Jake asked, each word more impatient than the other. He took a breath and tried to wait. Luke had been through a lot, too. Jake was amazed he'd been able to remember this much.

"Road out toward nowhere. Dark. Lost 'em."

"Lost the truck?"

Luke lifted his gaze to Jake. "Yeah. Then they found me."

"What happened next?" Jake asked, his need to know shouting loud and clear. Ella's hand on his arm told him that.

Luke slipped into sleep again but then he opened his eyes. "Turned off by the lake, drove around looking. Got hit from behind. Last I remember."

Then he opened his eyes wide and tried to get up. "Macey? Where's Macey?"

Jake held Luke down. "Whoa, hold on. You can't help right now. You need to rest and get well."

"Where is she?" Luke asked, his eyes wild now.

"She's still out there somewhere," Ella replied. "But we are going to find her," she quickly added.

Luke grunted in anger and despair. "I need to help. Couldn't save her. He tried to kill me."

A nurse hurried in the room before Luke could say anything more. "I'll give him something to calm him down," she said, a hand on Luke's pulse.

Ella shot Jake a glance then whispered, "Someone deliberately ran him off the road and into the lake."

Jake's head throbbed with anger. After the nurse left,

he said, "Can you remember anything about this person? Describe him or her?"

Luke swallowed, closed his eyes. "Black hoodie. All black...something covering his face when the truck went by the first time. Dark. Maybe a beard. Same as the person I saw today, right here."

"Tall, short, heavyset or slender?"

Luke glanced over at Ella. "Tall. Slender." He lay there for a minute and Jake wondered if he'd passed out completely. "I don't know...might have been..."

"Luke?"

The teenager went pale and quiet, his breathing becoming steady as he drifted back into a restful sleep brought on by the sedative.

Jake reached out to shake Luke back awake but Ella stopped him. "He's tired, Jake. And scared." She jotted notes on her phone notepad. "And he described the same type of person Macey's friend described. The same person I remember. Or someone dressed the same, at least." She patted Luke's still hand. "Seeing that person again today must have jarred some of his nightmares. He's given us a lot to work with."

"But he's drugged up and groggy," Jake said on a loud whisper. "What if he's just imagining things? What if he's confused?"

"I don't think he imagined seeing Macey or being run off the road. He must have gotten one good look at the kidnapper's hidden face, too."

Jake tried to piece things together. "How did her scarf get in his truck?"

Ella pulled him away from the bed. "The suspect obviously placed it there as another clue—and to scare us or make us think Luke was the culprit." She gave Luke a sympathetic glance. "The suspect left a clue on that scarf for us, so he knows we'd want to question Luke. I'm sure he's been prowling around the hospital waiting for Luke to wake up."

Jake touched a hand to his brow then glanced back over at Luke. "At least we can place the suspect—or someone matching his description—at the scene of Luke's wreck. And if Luke is credible, we have another eyewitness. We need to go back over that spot again."

"Jake, the forensics team has already done that."

"In those woods, it's easy to miss things."

He should know. He was supposed to be able to track just about anyone and yet he couldn't find a trace of his own daughter.

When they came out of Luke's room, his parents were there waiting.

"What did he say?" Bert Hurst asked, both fear and hope in his eyes.

Jake told them what he could. "Based on his comments, this is what I think happened. He went to the mall to see if Macey wanted a ride home until he thought he saw her in a truck, so he followed. He didn't say, but he must have thought she'd gotten a ride with someone else. The driver apparently sped away so Luke went after the truck and he thought he saw Macey inside."

He left out the details of how the driver had pushed her back down. He was too boiling-hot mad to even voice how he felt about that.

"Did he try to stop them?" Luke's mother asked.

"He lost the truck but apparently the driver waited for Luke."

Jake glanced at Ella then back at Luke's parents. "He implied the truck ran him off the road and into the lake. Luke must have hit his head either from the impact or maybe he fell after he got out of the truck. He might have been disoriented."

"He remembered all of that?" Bert asked, shock coloring his ruddy skin. "That's a good sign, at least."

Nadine gasped and put a hand to her mouth, her eyes watering. "He could have died out there. He could have drowned."

Ella put an arm around Nadine's shoulder. "Thankfully, that didn't happen. Luke's trying his best to tell us the truth and we're thanking God for that."

"So the same person who took Macey did this to our son," Bert said on a resolved note. "And came back here to finish the job."

"That's what we think," Jake replied. "We have to keep in mind that Luke suffered a trauma to his head. He's still a bit fuzzy about the details but he was pretty clear on the person he saw in his room."

"Then he must be telling you the truth," Nadine said, her voice insistent. "Luke didn't hurt Macey. He's trying to help."

"Yes," Ella replied, her eyes holding Jake's. "Yes, he's struggling, but we think seeing the same person again triggered some of his memory." She lowered her voice. "We have to keep this between us for now. We don't need reporters or overly interested friends speculating."

Luke's parents clung to each other, their expressions grim. Bert nodded. "We won't say a word."

"I'm putting extra guards on his room," Jake said, trying to reassure them. "And when I find the officer who walked away, he'll get an earful."

Nadine's head came up at that. "But we saw an officer right there just before this happened. Luke was never alone."

"Are you sure?" Ella asked, frowning.

Bert nodded. "We made sure, trust me. We've been here, right around the corner, just about the whole time, taking shifts sometimes and making sure someone was at that door even when friends came by."

"And you saw the guard there this morning?" Jake's gaze shifted from Luke's parents to the hospital room.

"Not the same one," Nadine said. "This was a new one. A young man." Her skin went pale. "Oh, my. Oh, no. You don't think—"

Jake pulled a hand down his face. "Ella, call the sheriff right away."

"I'm on it," Ella replied, her tone grim but firm.

Bert summed things up. "You think someone replaced the real guard? But where's the real one then?"

"That's what I'm about to find out," Jake replied. "Listen, stay right here and I'll alert the man I put on Luke's door."

He went into action, informing the hospital security staff that they had an officer missing and possibly down. Jake figured the guard had innocently accepted his replacement without verifying his identity. A bad mistake. At least the guard could still be alive.

But his burning gut told him otherwise. This sicko wouldn't leave anything to chance. He'd tried to kill Luke twice now. Jake wouldn't put it past him to try again. Or to kill anyone who stood in his way.

If he went to this much trouble to stop Luke, what would he do to Macey or Ella?

Jake couldn't go there. He wouldn't even think it.

He hurried through the corridors, searching, calling other officers, checking and rechecking. The whole hospital went into a security lockdown, everyone on high alert. Jake had to figure out how the suspect had lured the guard away without anyone noticing—and how he'd obviously dressed as an officer.

Then why did Luke say he was all in black? Nothing made sense right now.

It didn't take long for Jake to get a call from Ella.

"We've found the missing officer," she said, her voice raw and winded. "He's dead, Jake."

SIXTEEN

Back at the command center, Ella went over the clues in the case once again. They had one officer down. Too young to die so soon. Too much potential to be wasted at the hands of a madman. And they still didn't know the identity of the body they'd found near the old barn. In fact, other than Luke's description of the suspect and the possibility that the same person had been in his hospital room, they still had very little to go on.

"So we need to go back to the place where Luke's truck went into the water," she said to Jake. "Surely with the clues from the mural along with Luke's statement, we can put two and two together."

Jake didn't comment right away. He stood staring out at the woods, other task force officers mingling around him now that the official meeting was over. They'd had coffee and juice and a breakfast casserole prepared by Granny and several of her stoic, determined friends.

"We don't live in fear around here," her grandmother had reminded her as they served the casseroles. "And we are ever alert." Most of these ladies had permits to carry concealed weapons and they knew how to handle those weapons. They attended target practice at least once a month. This was Texas, after all.

Zip paced, the heightened tension fueling his need to

help. Ella patted his head now, wishing they could go for a walk around the perimeter like they used to do—what, a few days ago? Even on those walks, she'd carried protection.

Old habits died hard.

Funny, how life could change in a flash. She turned to stare at Jake. She's wasted a lot of time trying to run from him. And why? Did she want to be independent and strong? Did she believe he deserved better than her? Because their timing was never quite right?

Why did she push happiness away?

Maybe because her parents were happy together and they'd died that way? Together, loving, close.

And then gone in a flash.

Maybe because she'd come so close to death in a horrible way, that she was afraid to live life in an authentic way?

Was she scared of dying or was she scared of really living?

What is my problem, Lord? Can You help me figure that out, please? And while You're at it, can You please protect my family and friends...and Jake.

She'd been through a near-death experience. She should have learned from that. She should trust in the Lord and rejoice in a second chance.

"Ella?"

She blinked and found Jake standing there, giving her a look full of concern and yearning. "Sorry," she blurted. "I mean, I'm okay. Just...thinking."

His gaze danced over her face. "About what?"

"Wasted time," she retorted.

He didn't say anything but his eyes spoke to her with all the feelings he couldn't put into words. They went a dark, burning gold. "Ella..."

"Hey, Ranger Cavanaugh?"

The sheriff's loud call broke the moment and Jake

whirled around in a rush to get away. Away from her, away from the current of awareness that had burned between them like dry pine needles catching on fire. Away from whatever he'd been about to tell her.

Wasted time. She was wasting time now, Ella thought. She hurried back to the whiteboard so she could once again study the clues and the suspect's profile. What were they missing?

Jake listened to the sheriff, his heart pounding like a sledgehammer. He'd almost kissed Ella right here in the command center, with her granny cleaning up breakfast dishes nearby. He had to get his mind back on this case, back on Macey. "What did you say?"

Sheriff Steward gave him a worried stare. "I said we found a bedroom slipper down near the lake." The sheriff held up the paper bag. "Actually, Zip found it. Brought it right up to the door there."

Jake took the bag and looked inside. A dark blue moccasin-type slipper lay dirty and caked with mud. A moccasin? He'd wondered about that himself. He studied it a moment then looked back at the sheriff. "This doesn't look like a man's slipper."

"We know," the sheriff replied, his stern face filled with beard growth. "I'm thinking it must have belonged to the young girl we found."

"But we found her clear on the other side of the lake," Jake replied. A memory of those odd footprints in the mud and dirt passed through his mind. He'd seen the same footprints along the path the day he and Macey had followed one of the first clues. But the forensic team hadn't been able to make a solid impression. "How'd this get here?"

The sheriff nodded, rubbed at his left elbow with his right hand, a pained expression on his grizzled face. "We don't know. You're right about the young girl. Could be her slipper, since we found another slipper there in the old boat, near her body. I think it's a match for this one."

Jake blinked. "You think the killer had the girl here on Ella's property at one time."

"Looks that way."

Jake had to absorb this new development. "But why would he have her here?"

The sheriff leaned in. "Maybe he planned to kill her here, as a reminder to Ella. That poor girl has been dead for over a week or two, according to the medical examiner's initial assessment. Can't be clear until we get a full report."

Jake took off his hat and rubbed at his hair. "He must have dragged her all over the woods, same way he did Ella." He looked around to make sure Ella was still occupied. She stood staring at the white evidence board. "And he must have killed her a few days before he took Macey."

Had that girl been the sacrificial lamb, like the little kid goat the killer had left for them? Had he killed her to leave for Ella to find?

"Maybe he killed her somewhere around here, but panicked and moved her to that more secluded spot to make sure we'd find her if we found the mural."

"That's a possibility," the sheriff replied.

Jake nodded and handed the evidence bag back to the sheriff. "Thanks. I'm gonna talk to my fellow Rangers about this and maybe have another look at the site of Luke's crash." He'd already informed the team about questioning Luke. "Luke seems to think the person he saw this morning in his room is the same person who took Macey."

"And whoever it is," the sheriff responded, "he's getting desperate. I doubt he even realizes this slipper went missing."

"And that means Macey is in even more danger than ever," Jake replied, not even daring to state the worst. She could already be dead.

"I agree," the sheriff replied. His grim expression told Jake he was thinking along the same lines. "But don't give up, Jake. We're getting closer and closer. And he's getting sloppy."

Jake gave a curt nod. "I'll make sure everyone is aware of the slippers so we can compare them and I guess I'll do whatever I always do when a case has me stumped. I'll start at the beginning again."

"Good idea," the sheriff replied. Then he turned to snap his officers into action, assigning tasks to each member.

While Jake stood and stared out into the woods and wondered what he'd missed in all the clues.

"So what size is this slipper?" Ella asked later as they headed out to the woods again. Jake had told her what the sheriff's team had discovered on her property. While that scenario gave her the creeps, it also gave her hope that they were finally making headway.

"I don't know," Jake admitted. "But it wasn't a man's shoe. Maybe average. What size is that in women's shoes?"

"A seven or eight," she said, guessing. "Not too small but not to huge, either."

"That's about it then," he said. "A young girl could have been wearing those shoes."

Ella jotted notes in her phone app. "Or maybe the killer has small feet for a man and he was wearing them."

"But wouldn't they be hard to run in?" Jake asked.

"Not for an experienced runner," she said. "We should check around in running clubs and see what we find there, too."

Jake perked up at that and immediately called one of the Rangers to check into that. "So today, we go back over the crash site where we found Luke. And then we'll check with the church records you had the secretary pull up, right?"

"Right," Ella said. "She's working on that now—the

membership roster goes well back into the 1990s so we should have the picture directories they'd stored over the years."

"We have made a little progress but we can't pinpoint the house in the mural," Jake said, "I'm still worried. We're going on four days now and this killer gets antsy before a week goes by."

"Don't think about anything but finding Macey alive," Ella warned. "We should focus on that."

"That's all I do focus on," he said, "but I feel as if I'm just stuck in the mud, spinning out of control."

Ella glanced over at him, wishing she could ease some of his pain. She knew he had a lot on his mind—including her. Jake had always tried to protect her, to fight her battles before she herself could ever fight them. And while she admired that about him, it had also been a bone of contention between them.

It should still be, but right now she was so very glad he was here with her. "We're going to find her," Ella said, hoping the words sounded strong. "We will find her, Jake."

Jake gave her a quick glance then held his gaze toward the road ahead until they'd reached the dirt lane leading up to the old barn. "Here we go again," he said.

"Let's do a good search of the surrounding woods again since we were interrupted yesterday," Ella suggested. "At least we'll feel like we're doing something."

They locked up the truck, checked their weapons and headed out. "Nothing from the high school or any of the other places we've asked around," Jake said, his voice low and cautious.

"No, but you know how these things work. Someone might remember something or step forward. At least Luke is okay and he did give us a pretty good description and some other details that we can use."

They got out and glanced back over the mural. "Every

time I look at this thing, I see something else new," Ella said. "We need to search for the house since we didn't get a chance to yesterday morning."

They started out toward the woods. Based on the mural's depiction, a farmhouse should have been just west of the church. But the church in this picture was based on Ella's church, which was across the lake near the Louisiana border. No one had found an old farmhouse near the church so far.

While Jake scanned the tree line and the water, Ella scrolled through the pictures she'd taken yesterday. "You know, this house seems familiar to me," she said, a sick sensation warming her stomach. "Maybe I've seen it before in a picture or…somewhere around the lake."

Jake whirled and stomped back toward her. "Could the house be in another location, too?"

"Highly possible," Ella said. She studied the house. "It's white in the mural but I seem to remember a weathered wood. Probably why I didn't connect on that yesterday."

Jake let out a hiss. "Did he ever take off your blindfold?"

"No, not when he had me traipsing through the woods. It was part of keeping me disoriented and confused." She looked down at the decayed leaves underneath their feet. "He would sometimes take it off at night."

"Maybe you saw a picture in the old camp house where he kept you?"

An image flickered through Ella's mind, causing her to shut her eyes. "I don't know. I remember staring up and away. I think I was trying to come out of my body so I wouldn't have to deal with what he was doing to me."

She shut her photo app and put her phone away, her breath caught in her throat. "I've tried so hard to forget."

Jake was right there, holding her. "Don't think about it. If it comes, we'll see what it might mean. Don't force yourself."

Ella looked up at the pity in his eyes and pulled away. "I'm okay. I just think I've seen that house somewhere."

Jake's expression changed, an understanding passing through his expression. "You don't like talking about it, do you?"

"No. What woman would?" She busied herself with searching the distant shore where bald cypress trees covered with clinging Spanish moss huddled in cold, gray clumps against the murky greenish-black water.

Jake didn't push her. He turned back to study the woods. "I wish you'd told me, Ella."

"I'm telling you now."

He let it go at that. "Whenever you're ready…"

"I know," she said on a rush. "Let's check the woods."

They followed an old dirt lane around a copse of cluttered trees. Ella searched the treetops and the scrub oaks and tried to squint into the dense thickets beyond. "If there was a house here, the forest has taken it over."

They trudged into the woods, Jake leading the way. Memories swirled around Ella like gnats and mosquitoes, buzzing inside her head with a dull roar. Where had she seen that house?

About thirty minutes into their trek, perspiration pooled between her shoulder blades in spite of the chilly day. They'd trudged through bushes and brush, pushed away cobwebs and stepped around dormant fire ant beds. And they hadn't seen any buildings or outbuildings.

"Maybe we should turn around," she called out to Jake as the sun climbed in the sky. "We have to go back by the church, remember?"

Jake waved a hand. "Okay. Let me just see—"

When he stopped talking, Ella hurried the few yards between them. "What is it?"

Jake put a finger to his lips and motioned to her to stay quiet. Ella slowed her steps and did a double check of their surroundings. When she reached Jake, he pointed to what looked like a door sticking out of a mound that had been hidden by shrubs and palmetto palms.

Ella's heart lurched and crashed, adrenaline rushing over her. She glanced at the old door and then back to Jake. "A mine?"

"Or an old root cellar," he whispered. He leaned down, his ear against the thick, gray wood. "I don't know. Can't hear a thing."

"Should we open it?" she asked.

"I plan to open it," he replied.

"Let me call for backup."

"No time."

She knew that tone. Jake thought his daughter might be behind this door. She couldn't blame him for wanting to get inside. And true to form, most Rangers did what they wanted to do when it came to finding criminals.

She nodded. "Hurry. I'll be your lookout."

"Fine, but only until I get the door open. You're not leaving my sight."

He holstered his gun and went about trying to open the door. A few grunts later, he stood and shook his head. "Heavy and rusty."

"We can get someone out here."

Jake glanced around, then found an old limb. "Let me try to pry it open with this."

Ella waited, checking and rechecking every creak, rustle and crack she heard reverberating through the woods. Glancing back at Jake, she watched as he wedged the old limb against the door's rusted metal handle and tried to pry it open. The limb broke in two and sent him sprawling back. Jake hit her with a grunt and brought her down with him.

The next thing Ella knew, she was on the ground with

Jake over her, their gazes locked together as they stared into each other's eyes.

And then, they heard gunshots and Jake spread his body across hers and held her, covering her from the ping-ping of bullets whizzing all around them.

SEVENTEEN

"Stay down!" Jake whispered the command against Ella's ear, then lifted his head above the cover of the mound. He doubted she'd listen, but he didn't wait to see. Squinting into the sunlight, he tried to get a bead on the shooter.

Another round of lead whizzed by, hitting trees and shrubs just inches away. "They have us in their sights," he said to Ella as he slid back beside her. "And right now, we don't have a way out." He gave her a quick once-over. "Are you okay?"

"I'm fine," she replied as she scooted closer to the old door. "Somebody doesn't want us to see what's inside here."

"That isn't gonna stop me," Jake retorted, his back pressed against the dirt mound. "I'll shoot out the lock if I have to."

"And how do you plan to do that if you're being shot at, too?"

He mulled that over. "Haven't figured that one out yet."

"I can cover you," she suggested, getting busy as she checked her rifle.

"No. Too dangerous."

"Jake, we don't have time to argue. Someone is trying to kill us."

Jake glanced around, looking for escape routes. "We

came from the south," he reasoned. "So they must have been on our trail for a while. Either that or they stumbled upon us and started shooting."

"So they came from the road, same as we did?"

"Hard to say. I don't think a wanted criminal would travel the road." He squinted into the trees. "But they could have tracked us through the woods."

Ella did a visual of the area. "We might have missed another trail. We searched about a mile farther than the team went yesterday. They stopped when they found the dead girl."

"We'll need to carve a new trail to get out of here."

"Or we could do as I suggested and call for backup."

Jake couldn't argue with that, since his main goal was to open this door. "Okay, have it your way."

Ella didn't waste time with a retort. She called in their location and explained the situation. "One shooter, we think."

Then she turned to Jake. "Posse's on the way."

Jake stared at her, then glanced back at the door. "I want in there."

"Don't even think about it," she said. "You could get shot. You need to wait for help."

She was right, of course. They were pinned down for now.

But he could test that theory. He shifted and peeked over a cluster of winter-dry bramble.

Another shot rang out.

"Looks like we'll be here awhile," Ella said on a smug note. "You'll just have to calm down and twiddle your thumbs for a while."

"I'm not the thumb-twiddling type."

Ella gave him a wry stare. "Really?"

"I can at least check for signs of tracks," he replied, impatience in every word. Glancing around, he noted a few broken twigs here and there but no clear path to and from the old cellar. "Probably nobody's been here," he finally said. "I don't see any way someone's been in this place. The door is solid and stuck."

"It's worth checking," Ella said on a low whisper while she watched the woods for any approaching shooters. "Everything is worth checking."

"I agree. If Macey's in there…"

"We'll get her out," Ella finished before he could say anything worse. "But we can't do it alone right now."

Jake glared at the gray-washed wood, his gaze hitting on anything out of the ordinary that he might have missed in his haste to get the door open. When he spotted a strand of faded red caught against an old hinge, he motioned to Ella. "Look at that."

Ella twisted around, her gaze moving over the old door. "A hair ribbon…or possibly the same kind of fibers we found on the goat and the female body?" She glanced back at Jake. "Do you remember if Macey was wearing anything red when she got taken?"

Jake shook his head. "She had her hair down that morning, but you know girls tend to change their hairstyles during any given day."

Ella's smile was indulgent. "Yeah, I do know that. Maybe she put it up in gym class and left it."

"I don't know," he said, his eyes on the ribbon. "It's faded out a bit. She had on that scarf we found in Luke's truck, but I don't recall her wearing anything red."

Ella gave it one more glance. "I think I can snag it so we can have a closer look."

She reached up, but a round of gunfire greeted her.

Jake yanked her arm down. "Don't do that again."

"Sorry." She slinked low, her head pressing against dry earth. "I guess we'll have to wait for reinforcements." Then she nudged him. "You know, that fabric could *belong* to our Jane Doe. If it's got a loose hair on it, we might have a chance at DNA so we can identify that poor girl."

"It's something," he said, his mind circling around what they might find down in this hole. "I hate having to sit still." He shimmied down on his belly and adjusted his sunglasses. "At least I can try to find out where the shots are coming from."

Ella did the same, her eyes on the distant trees. "What if he's gone?"

"Then we'll be able to open this door."

Jake scanned the trees, watching for any movement. When something flashed a few yards away, he nudged Ella. "Movement at your two o'clock."

Ella glanced to the right and took a breath. "I see one shooter, moving south toward our location."

"He's wearing an orange hunting vest," Jake replied. "Surely he doesn't think we're deer."

"He might be wearing it on purpose, to blend in if he's questioned by the game warden or anyone else."

"Of course. Hiding in plain sight seems to be his MO." Jake shifted and turned his head toward Ella. "We need to confront him."

She shook her head. "No."

"We're wasting time, Ella."

She slanted him a look that told him she remembered their earlier conversation. "Why do you insist on going it alone, Jake? Why do you roll over everyone and put your own life in danger?"

"It's my job," he retorted, anger coloring each word. "And it's *my* daughter."

"Well, if you aren't careful, Macey could lose both her parents."

Jake went still and watched as Ella's mouth dropped open. "I'm so sorry," she said on a low whisper. "Jake…"

"Come out with your hands up, right now."

Jake didn't have time to think about Ella's harsh suggestion, but he knew she had a point. And because he didn't want to think about that right now, he pulled out his badge and held it in the air. "Texas Ranger. I suggest you drop that weapon and tell us why you're shooting at us."

Ella couldn't stop thinking about what she'd said to Jake earlier. She sat on the back of a Sheriff Department cruiser, watching as the woods filled with law officials.

The man shooting at them had a strong alibi and a fairly good reason for what he'd done.

"I'm sick and tired of trespassers on my land," he'd explained after Jake had shown his badge. "Kids always hanging out back here, skinny-dipping in the lake, drinking and carrying on. I've told the county over and over that this old root cellar is back here. Used to be a house here, too. I guess they used it for a storm shelter. But now it's a danger and nobody'll do anything about it and I got teenagers who could get hurt or killed if they mess with the thing and try to go down in it."

"So you decided to take the law into your own hands?" Ella asked, her gun trained on the now-afraid old man.

"I just wanted to scare y'all away," the man said on a gravelly whine. "Don't like trespassers." He pointed back toward where they'd trekked through the woods. "Get enough of tourists coming to see that old mural some prankster painted on the side of that barn a few miles east of here."

"Do you know who that prankster might be?" Jake asked while sirens wailed in the background. "We're looking for a possible kidnapper."

And so it had gone. The man—Mr. Jenkins—didn't know who'd painted the mural since it had been there when he bought the land at a foreclosure sale. But he didn't like the attention it had brought to his twenty acres of land. By the time backup had arrived, he was sweating and swearing and hoping he wouldn't be put in jail for trying to shoot a Texas Ranger. But he had said one thing that had sent chills down Ella's back.

"I patrol these woods day and night. A few nights ago, I swear I heard a girl scream out here. Never found anything, though. Coulda been an animal or something. Just shot in the air to scare 'em away." The old man had stomped and shuffled his brogans in the dirt. "Then I heard about a girl gone missing and…I wondered…if I could have helped. What if that's the girl I heard?"

Ella and Jake had questioned him over and over and so had the sheriff, but he couldn't identify anyone. "I didn't even hear a car crank up or anyone moving through the woods. But I know somebody was out here." His gaze had hit on the old door. "Thought it might be the same people again today."

Jake hadn't said a word after that. His face had turned ashen and his mood had turned black. He'd grabbed the first officer on the scene and demanded they get that door pried open.

Ella wanted that, too, but Jake wasn't communicating with her right now. She watched as he stomped back and forth and conferred with several others, but he refused to even glance her way.

What had she been thinking, telling him that Macey would be alone if she lost him? It was true, but did she have to be so brutal at a time when he needed her to be supportive and compassionate? She was those things, but the man was so stubborn and he made her so angry and worried and fretful that she just lost most of her sensible cells and blurted out the worst possible words to say to a worried, grieving daddy.

"Jake?" She stood as he rushed by. "Jake, what's going on?"

He turned and gave her a hard stare. "Nothing." Then he took off toward the new path they'd formed through the woods.

Finally, tired of staying out of the way, Ella hurried behind him to the spot where they'd found the cellar door.

The sheriff had it open now and a forensic team had been called in to investigate. She shuddered to think what might be behind that door.

"Jake?"

"Not now, Ella." He bumped past her, his back straight, his expression tightly held in a tense frown.

Dear God, don't let Macey be dead down there.

Ella repeated the frantic prayer then calmly stilled her heart. No matter what they found, no matter what happened from here on out, she had to rely on the Lord to guide her.

And she had to let Jake be Jake. She well remembered his stubborn streak and his tremendous pride. And she also remembered how they'd butted heads more than once.

Maybe they didn't have a second chance or any chance of making it together, but she wouldn't let that stop her from helping Jake.

He needed her, even if he couldn't admit that right now.

So she followed him toward the old cellar door and watched, her breath caught in her throat, as several men lifted the door back and then stood with flashlights, waiting for the sheriff and Jake to go down.

Jake finally looked up and glanced toward Ella, his expression bordering on desperation and heartbreak. She wanted to run to him and hold him back so she could go down there first. So she could prepare him, comfort him, help him.

But Jake turned and lowered himself down into the gray, open earth so Ella waited with all the others, her prayers scattering out over the sunny, cold sky like dry leaves twirling in the wind.

EIGHTEEN

Jake checked his weapon and followed the sheriff's deputy and a couple of other officers into the old cellar, his boots hitting against the brittle, dirt-covered wooden steps that had been crudely carved into the earth. A high-powered flashlight beam shot out an eerie glow over the long narrow space. Jake dreaded looking past the beam's yellow-washed light but he had to know the truth.

Was Macey lying here, alone? And alive? Or dead?

He stood back at first, waiting for any word from the sheriff. But after a few seconds of silence, Jake rushed forward and stared into the dark dungeon-like space.

"Clear," the sheriff called, his hand holding Jake back.

But Jake could see that the dark, moldy place was empty.

And cold. So cold.

"Someone was held here," Jake finally said, his heart doing a heavy bumping all around his insides. He could hear his pulse vibrating inside his head. "But nothing now. Nothing."

"And no one," Sheriff Steward said on a blunt note. "I'm sorry, Jake. But this doesn't mean anything yet. We have to hold out hope."

Jake motioned with one hand. "May I take the light, sir?"

The robust sheriff nodded to his deputy and the young

man handed the light to Jake. He held it over his raised gun and moved it around as if he were seeking buried treasure. But the treasure he needed to find wasn't here. He didn't know whether to laugh in relief or cry out in frustration. "We found that piece of red ribbon," he said, his eyes following the flashlight's beam. "I had hoped to find more evidence here."

He shifted, letting the light dance over the dark, damp walls. Jake took in the scents of mold, dust and decay, breathing deep while he studied the walls and the floor. After a few moments, he caught another scent. Perfume.

"I smell a woman's perfume," he said, spinning on his boots to see into the dark recesses of the space.

"Over there," the sheriff said, pointing to a deep corner. "I thought I saw something, a piece of clothing maybe."

Jake hurried to the corner, the sheriff right behind him.

A red scarf lay among the trash and leaves on the old dirt floor.

"Red," he said. "Not Macey's." He glanced back at the sheriff. "So we have red fibers found at two crime scenes and now on the door here. Could they all be from this one scarf?"

"We'll search every corner," the sheriff said. "We might stumble on something else."

Jake agreed with that. "I wonder if Macey was ever held here. It seems he might have used this spot but moved on when Mr. Jenkins started getting too close."

The sheriff nodded. "I'm surprised he didn't try to kill that stubborn old man. But then, Jenkins seems to know his way around a weapon and a high-powered rifle might scare anyone away."

Jake nodded. "I guess I should be glad Jenkins fired at us. His statement can be filed to help us build a case at least."

Sheriff Steward shot a glance into the dark. "We have to establish that the suspect—whoever that is—was here at one time. And I'm not sure how that's gonna pan out."

"Like you said, we follow the evidence."

"Every little bit helps," the sheriff said. "You know that, Jake. The more we find, the more we can thread together to make a case once we find this perpetrator."

"If we ever do."

Jake did another search and saw more trash piles here and there. He'd wait for the forensic team before he helped to shuffle through those. Hopefully, they'd find something else to add to the growing list of evidence. Would that evidence lead them to the Dead Drop Killer and to Macey? He prayed so.

When he emerged back into the daylight, the sun was high in the sky but a chilling wind blew a mournful wail through the woods and out over the distant lake. He lifted his head and searched the area. Ella was sitting on the tailgate of his pickup. She glanced up and into his eyes, her expression full of hope and pain.

Jake wanted to stay mad at her about what she'd said earlier, but he couldn't. She'd been by his side for days now, with very little food or sleep. They were both exhausted, but he shouldn't be blaming her for any of this. She'd been through more than one woman should have to bear, and he'd seen how shattered she'd become after being taken by the killer.

And yet she'd survived because she was strong and smart and...because Ella had a fierce need to keep fighting. She'd fought through her grief after her parents had been so tragically killed and she'd fought her way back to life after being held for two long weeks in these woods. Ella had always been a fighter. But he'd never truly realized that until right now, right this minute.

All this time, he'd considered her as someone who ran away from any type of emotional confrontation, but he'd been so wrong on that. Ella met confrontation head-on and figured out a way around it. Especially the emotional kind.

While he stood still and fought against his feelings with a stubborn streak that only brought him grief and left him standing alone. He'd done that with Ella from the start and she'd mowed right over him and kept right on going. He'd tried that with Natalie and she'd let him rant while she'd silently and diligently gone about loving him and their daughter. And while she'd silently become too sick to survive.

Left with tremendous guilt, Jake now wondered why any woman would want to put up with him. Had he treated Macey that way, too, in his need to protect her and love her?

Maybe he needed to stop being so self-righteous and stubborn. It might be time to change his mind-set and accept that it was okay to love a strong, self-reliant woman.

Love? Did he still love Ella?

Jake couldn't deal with that right now.

He couldn't do anything until he had Macey home again.

Because, unlike Ella, if he lost his daughter, too, he might not be able to push through to the other side. He might not ever come back from that brink. So instead of apologizing to Ella, he walked back to the cluster of officers and continued to help with the investigation, bagging and cataloguing evidence and discussing the ifs, ands and buts of this case. When they were through, he turned and saw that Ella wasn't sitting on the tailgate anymore.

He didn't see her anywhere at all.

Ella stood staring out at the lake, the sparkle of sunshine that shimmered on the water making her eyes see spots. She was thankful that they hadn't found Macey inside that dark deep hole, but now she was worried that they might not find the girl.

Jake would never get over that. He'd gone beyond the

call of duty to the ultimate duty of being a father. He wouldn't give up until he knew one way or another. He'd have a hard time if the worst happened.

And he wouldn't give in to his feelings for Ella until he found Macey. Maybe not even after he found Macey. The man was a walking testament to the strong, silent type. He expected the traditional values he'd grown up with and she respected that. Ella had the same values, but she also had a solid sense of justice and that had carried her through to becoming one of the best FBI agents in the state of Texas.

It would carry her through now, too.

She wanted to find Macey as much as Jake did, but they couldn't do it if they were bickering and circling and trying to deny the attraction that they'd always had for each other.

So she was going to take herself off this case.

She'd stay close, man the command center and the tip lines and help with meals for the task force and volunteers. She'd continue to gather the clues and evidence and try to find a solution to this puzzle. But she wasn't going to ride shotgun with Jake anymore.

Too close for comfort in oh so many ways.

Having decided that, she felt at peace for the first time in days. But when she turned and found him stalking toward her, that peace disappeared like fog over the lake.

"Where have you been?"

Assessing his anger, Ella put her hands on her hips. "Right here."

He pulled his hat off and adjusted the collar of his navy, lightweight, Texas Ranger–embossed jacket. "Ella, you know not to wander off like that."

"Wander off?" She would have laughed if this hadn't been such a serious situation. "I didn't wander off. I walked out to the water to think, to find some alone time. I was always within sight of everything and everyone."

"I couldn't find you," he said on a breath that seemed to catch in his throat.

A breath that caught at her heart.

Ella lowered her head but lifted her gaze to look up at him. "I'm sorry. I needed some space. I've been thinking—"

"I don't want to hear any apologies for what you said earlier. I know you meant well and you were right. I need to be mindful that if something happens to me, Macey will be all alone. I need to consider everything."

Was he considering how he might wind up alone, too?

She picked up on his tone but refused to be angry back at him. "I've been considering everything, too, Jake. And I think I've done all I can for you on this case—"

"What?"

The shock on his face held her. "I'm not abandoning you, but I think I'd do better staying close to the command center and watching over the phones and directing the volunteers. I can still study the evidence and the patterns and maybe come up with something concrete to help you."

"And who'll help watch out for you? I don't have time—"

"You don't need to worry about me. I'll have people around me and things will just be better without me hindering you. You're good at your job, Jake. I don't want to be a distraction."

He stared at her, his eyes sweeping over her face in a gaze of sweetness and regret. "You've had enough, right?"

Never enough.

Ella didn't answer that question. "I made you angry earlier and I'm apologizing. I said a horrible thing and I'm sorry. But I don't want anything to happen to you. So I think I need to give you the space you need to find your daughter."

He didn't spout out the usual words of concern. Maybe

he saw the logic of this decision, too. He had to accept that they might never be together again. And she had to do the same.

"It's better this way, Jake."

Finally, he slung his hat low over his brow and nodded. "We need to get you home."

And with that he turned and headed back to the cluster of people still milling around in the woods.

Ella followed, disappointment warring with her common sense.

Jake would consider her actions as another rejection of him. But he would be so wrong on that. She was trying to save him and help him. Because if he couldn't find his daughter, he would never be able to return the love Ella held for him in that compartment in the corner of her heart. He'd resent her for everything. And that would be *her* undoing.

The ride back to her place started out quietly. Jake drove, his face etched in lines and shadows, his silence etched in regret and remorse.

"I hope y'all found something to give us a break," Ella said to ease the silence. "The red ribbon might hold some answers."

"Yep."

Okay, he was back to that again. His one-word comments always spoke more than she needed to know.

"I can do some research. Get online and follow some clues or run down some leads. Whatever I can do."

"Fine."

She tried again. "Jake, it's a good sign that Macey wasn't down there. I mean, that we didn't find anyone down there."

"Okay."

"It could mean he was never there with anyone."

"Right."

Ella stared at the long slants of sun moving over the countryside. This had been a long day. She just wanted a shower and a meal and, maybe, some sleep. But how could she sleep? How could either of them sleep?

She turned to stare over at Jake. Beard shadow darkened his jawline and his hair curled against his hat and the collar of his jacket. Ella wanted to reach out her hand to touch the rough growth on his face or maybe to push at that rogue hair trying to entice her. She sat in her corner, watching him, wishing things for him, for them. Things that probably would never happen.

When he turned the truck into the compound, Ella was more than ready to hop out and hurry to the house. But Jake's hand on her arm stopped her.

His gaze washed over her face in a golden heat. "You know, Ella, if you want to stop distracting me, then don't ever look at me that way again."

"What way?" she said on a dare, awareness coloring her skin pink.

He leaned in, his tawny-colored eyes rivaling the last of the rich, molten sunrays. "You know what I'm talking about," he said on a husky growl. "We're not near finished with each other."

Ella lifted away from his touch. "But we are finished for now," she said on a hoarse whisper. "I'm sorry but it has to be this way."

Then she got out of the truck and ran toward the shelter of her home.

NINETEEN

"Honey, you look plum beat."

Ella nodded toward her grandmother Edna. "I am, Granny. Tired, bone-weary, worried, irritated. You name it, I'm feeling it right now."

Granny gave her an indulgent smile. "Does Jake Cavanaugh have anything to do with all that?"

Ella blinked back the tears forming in her eyes. She would not humiliate herself by crying right here in the Caddo Country kitchen. "A little," she admitted after checking to make sure Jake wasn't close by. "But mostly, I'm just worried about Macey. It's been five days now, but it seems like a lifetime."

Edna kept peeling potatoes. "The two go hand in hand. He's a worried father and…you still care about him."

"Yes, I do," Ella said. She went about stirring the beef they'd put into a large pot hours ago for stew. Now that the beef was tender and browned to perfection, they'd started adding the other ingredients. Onions and green peppers sizzled, sending up a puff of good-smelling steam. "I care about both of them and it's so hard not to do more."

"You can't do much more," Granny replied. She dropped the potatoes into the pot and watched as Ella started stirring them until they were covered in the rich brown gravy.

"You're still in danger, so I think it's good that you've decided to step back from this investigation."

Ella had blurted that part to her grandmother the minute she'd come into the kitchen. Granny Edna always saw through her and found the truth, so Ella had learned to confide in her grandmother. She always considered Granny's advice as just what she needed. But she wanted her to understand, too.

She tossed a few sprigs of rosemary into the stew. "I'm still involved. I'll just be here more now than out there," she explained. "I can accomplish a lot by studying the clues and what little information we've put together."

"You'll be guarded, right?"

Ella nodded, then lifted a thumb to point to the porch. "Guards on each side of the house and out on the perimeter. Yes, ma'am."

"Good." Granny poured vegetable broth into the soup pot and turned down the heat. "Let's let that simmer a bit and then I'll thicken it back into gravy. Biscuits should be just right with this. It's getting cold out there tonight."

Ella shivered in spite of herself. Cold and dark and scary for a young girl all alone with a madman. "I'll make some tea and later we'll get a pot of coffee brewing to go with those blondies the staff made earlier."

She glanced down at the messages her grandparents and some of the volunteers had jotted on a notebook by the phone. One from the church secretary, wondering why she hadn't come by to look at the old directories. She'd call and reschedule that for tomorrow, since they hadn't been able to get by there today. Ella glanced at the next message. "The Festival Committee chair called again?"

Granny nodded. "Yes, for about the tenth time today. They're concerned that you won't be giving tours or holding dinners during the festival this weekend. I tried to explain that you're consulting on this case, but you know how some people are."

"I sure do," Ella replied. "I'll call Judith back and explain things to her in a way she can understand."

Granny chuckled and went back to her work.

Ella wondered if a little honey might be better than her blunt discussions with Jake. Then again, that man wouldn't fall for any honeyed words. He liked honest and forthright women. Ella had been honest, all right. Honest enough to send him away at least twice now.

Make that three times if she counted this latest one.

After checking the stew, she sat down at the old rolltop desk in the back part of the big, long industrial kitchen and started returning calls.

"Judith, it's Ella. Got your message. I hope you realize that with this investigation ongoing, I can't possibly open Caddo Country during the Christmas Festival."

She heard Judith rustling papers. "I thought you gave up this kind of dangerous work," Judith retorted. "Why on earth do you want to be a part of this investigation, anyway?"

"I'm consulting," Ella replied and left it at that.

"I understand," Judith said on a sigh. "You just hear all kinds of things around here. Seems to me, no matter how serious this is, you don't have any business being involved. You need to get back to work and help us make this festival a success. Let the local police and the sheriff take care of this."

Molten heat seared Ella's skin. "Let me be very clear, Judith. I am not opening Caddo Country during the Christmas Festival. I'm helping out on this case because a dear friend came to me for help in finding his daughter, and frankly, anything beyond that is none of your business."

"I'm just worried," Judith said on a huff. "I guess you

have to do what you need to do, but you'll be letting down a lot of people."

"I'd be letting down someone very important to me if I don't help with this," Ella said. "And that's a scared young girl who could be out there somewhere with a killer."

Judith didn't respond at first. But finally she cleared her throat and spoke, her tone less skeptical. "I suppose you have a point. I've heard about your ordeal and I don't mean to belittle that at all."

"This isn't about me." Ella refused to discuss with Judith what she'd gone through five years ago. It wouldn't matter, anyway. Judith didn't care about that right now. She only cared about this all-important festival and the dollars it would bring the area surrounding Caddo Lake.

But Ella had more on her mind right now than economic impact. "I've contributed to this festival for the last few years, but if you can't understand why I'm doing this, I'll stop contributing period. Got it?"

"Okay, all right," Judith replied. "I didn't mean to get you all riled up. You go on and do what you can. But we'll sure miss you being a part of things."

Ella started to ask Judith to reconsider even having the festival, but it was a big deal and it was spread out over two counties. Not something that could be stopped so close to the opening date. "Just be on alert," she said. "Make sure you have enough officers to watch out for the crowds."

"We always do," Judith said. "Thanks for calling me back, Ella."

Ella ended the call, then let out a frustrated groan.

"Wow, you sure told her good."

She turned to find Jake leaning against the wide archway between the kitchen and the small office, his expression haggard and full of fatigue even while a wry smile colored his face.

Swallowing the need to walk right into his embrace,

she said, "Some people just don't get things the first time. Have to be told over and over."

He came in and sat down in a straight-backed chair across from her. "You can count me among that category, I reckon."

Ella glanced at the pile of messages she still needed to sort through. "Everything okay?" she asked, deciding comparing their flaws might not be a good idea right now.

He braced one booted foot across the knee of his other leg, his jeans stretching over his thigh. "We've heard back on some of the lab reports."

Her heart did a little flip. "And?"

"The slippers don't show any signs of DNA so we can't match them to the Jane Doe. But the red fibers found on her body and in the boat are a match to the material we found on the little goat and on the cellar door. Part of the scarf we found inside. So that puts her inside the cellar at one time and the matched pair of slippers puts her here— or at least someone with her was here. She was probably moved to the boat…after she died."

Ella shut her eyes to that horror. Had the unnamed girl died here? "Poor girl. Any word on who she might be?"

"No." He held a hand to the foot pressed across his knee. "We're thinking she could be a runaway but nobody's come forward to report her as missing. We're putting her picture out for the media and hoping maybe someone will recognize her."

"Next best step," Ella replied. She nodded toward the big dining room where the task force members were gathering for dinner. "Is the task force meeting after supper?"

"Yep. Will you attend?"

That question held a lot of little question marks that couldn't be answered right now. "Of course. I told you I'd stay on top of things here and work the command center." She pointed to the stack of messages. "Beginning with these. All kind of calls coming in right now." She offered to go to the church first thing in the morning to glance at the directories.

"Don't leave here without an escort." His gaze flickered over the notes. "I'll let you get back to it then. Just wanted to give you the latest."

"I appreciate that," she said, thinking this new polite awkwardness was hard to handle. But not as hard as being alone with him all hours of the day. To hide her discomfort, she read through the papers in her hand, her gaze scanning each message.

Jake stood. "I'm going back to talk to some of the other officers. See you in a bit."

"Okay." Ella's gaze hit on the note in her hand and her heart stopped and shorted out. "Oh, wait. Jake?"

He was right there in two quick steps. "What is it?"

She showed him the message someone had taken down.

Jake read it out loud. "Tell Ella I'm thinking about her. She always was a strong girl and now she's a strong woman. Like an unseen angel."

Jake yanked the paper out of her hand and reread it. Underneath the message, one of the volunteers had jotted, Didn't leave a number.

Jake's gaze slammed into hers. "Do you think it was him?"

Ella's blood turned cold. "Who else would be so bold? *Unseen angel*—that's part of the lyrics of the hymn, remember?"

"I remember," he said. "He's still messing with us."

"But what is his reasoning? What does he plan to do next? That's what we have to figure out."

Jake wadded up the paper, then pulled it back apart. "He still has Macey and we can only pray he doesn't do anything to her."

"He wants me," Ella said, thinking she'd known this all along. "Why don't we let him have me?"

"No," Jake replied, his eyes burning a hot bronze. "No, Ella. We've talked about this. You need to stay here inside this house with guards around you. I mean that. Just let me do my job and promise me you won't do anything on your own."

"So now I'm a prisoner in my own home."

"No. But you'll be safe here, surrounded by people who can watch out for you."

She got up and looked into Jake's eyes. "We both know that if he wants me, he'll get to me. It's only a matter of time."

"I won't let him do that."

"You need to focus on finding Macey, remember?"

He slapped the back of the desk chair. "How can I forget?" Shaking his head, he turned. "I need to give this note to the sheriff. And you need to stick close to this house." Stomping back into the office, he added, "Let someone else search those church directories. Or have them delivered here."

"Okay," she said to calm him. "I'll be careful, Jake. I don't want to go through that again. Trust me."

But she would if it meant finding Macey alive.

Jake nodded, a darkness churning in his eyes. He had to be thinking about Macey.

Ella tried to tug him back to business. "I'll be out in little while to help with supper and to sit in on the briefing."

"When we're done, I'll escort you between here and the house."

"Jake?"

"Don't fight me on this, Ella. You might think by backing off you can stop me from caring, but that will never happen." He gave her one last glance then whirled around and headed off across the long kitchen.

Ella stood there against the doorframe, her heart caught in a trap full of need and longing. Then she thought about the message she'd just read. She needed to find out who'd taken that message and why that person hadn't found it suspicious.

If she kept her mind on that instead of Jake, they'd all be better off and she might be able to save Macey. At least she could do that for Jake, if nothing else.

TWENTY

Ella had both the box of church directories and the expansive volunteer list in front of her. She sat in the den with her grandparents and Zip nearby. They'd served breakfast to some of the guards and earlier shift workers so now she was settled in for the morning. It felt good to be back here where she felt safe and loved.

But she missed Jake already.

Letting out a yawn, she covered her mouth with her hand. "Excuse me," she said to her grandparents. Zip lifted his head to give her a doleful glance before he shifted into a more comfortable napping position.

"You're not getting much sleep," Grandpa said on a sour note, his bifocals down on his nose. "I'm sure glad you wised up and decided to stick around the house. We got plenty of folks out there on the job. They know what they're doing."

Ella gave him an indulgent smile and decided not to remind him she'd once been one of those people. "And I'm doing my part right here," she said, a hand on the stack of old directories. So I'd better get cracking."

"Want me to help?" Granny offered with a much softer tone than her husband's. She deftly kept right on knitting one of her fuzzy scarves. Her actions made Ella think about the tattered red scarf they'd found in the old cellar. Determination pushed her back on task.

"I might need you to help me remember some of these people," Ella replied, her hand on the latest directory. "But I'll let you know when and if I need you."

"I'll be puttering around," Granny replied. "Just give me a holler."

Ella nodded and took a sip of her coffee. She'd seen Jake earlier at breakfast but he'd left with the sheriff to check all the parks around the lake, a task that could easily take all day. They'd established the perpetrator had to be hanging out at popular teen sites—cruising roads and back roads, boat docks and landings and the public beaches. Maybe they'd pick up a trail somewhere out there.

And she hoped to pick up her own trail in one or maybe both of these two different sources. Ella started with the directories, deciding she'd work between the two to break up the monotony. But after going over two directories and one page of the ten-page volunteer sign-in list, her eyes were becoming bleary.

"Tired, honey?" Granny came by with a couple of chocolate chip cookies and a fresh pot of coffee. "Mid-morning snack."

Ella smiled up at her grandmother and bit into one of the still-warm cookies. "My eyes are glazing over but I'm seeing faces I'd kind of forgotten."

"Maybe one of them will help you remember something."

Taking a sip of the steaming coffee, Ella chewed then turned to her grandmother. "Granny, do you remember teaching anyone in Sunday School who was talented in art? Or maybe knowing a teenager who attended youth group who was an artist?"

Her grandmother put the coffee away and came back with her own cup to settle down in a rocker next to the table where Ella worked. "Hmm, my mind isn't as good as it used to be and we had several talented children passing through, including you."

Ella rolled her eyes on that one. "I only sang the one time in church, then a few times at weddings and things."

"But you have a lovely voice," Granny pointed out with pride. "I remember how proud we were that Sunday. Just wish your mama and daddy could have been there to hear you." She gave Ella a quiet smile. "But they could hear— even way up there in heaven. You sounded like an angel. At least we got a good picture of you for that year's directory."

A chill went down Ella's spine. "I was fifteen, so that year's directory should be here. That would be around twenty years ago."

She lifted directories until she found one with the dates for that time, then, her hands shaking, she started searching for the picture of her singing that her grandmother had mentioned. She might be able to find shots of the audience there, too.

When she saw a group of pictures in the back of the directory featuring the children and youth of the church, her heart wobbled but she held steady with a prayer.

Granny Edna went to get up, but Ella stopped her. "Hold on. I want you to look at these pictures, too."

"Okay." Edna leaned in, her big glasses reflecting the light from the lamp. "Who are we looking for?"

"Any youth or young adult who you might remember as being an artist. Or maybe a little out there? Weird, maybe?"

Granny nodded and studied the grainy pictures. "Well, I sure remember you." Her gaze moved from Ella standing alone in front of the choir to a few pictures of other youths sitting in a prominent spot in the front pews. "It was Youth Sunday, I believe. Several others showed off their talents, too."

"Any artists among the bunch?" Ella asked, her pulse bumping against her temple.

Granny studied the grinning young people and pointed to a few. "Well, he went on to play college baseball and this one is a nurse over in Tyler at the medical center and I do believe the boy sitting by her works in Washington, now. Can you imagine that?"

"Anything else?" Ella asked, trying to be patient.

Her grandmother's eyes moved over the pages. "I don't recall any of this group being artists, honey." She gave Ella an apologetic glance. "I'm sorry I can't be more help."

Ella studied the pictures, thinking she didn't really remember much herself. Except Jake, of course. He'd come to hear her sing that day. She pointed to where he sat back behind the other youth. "Look at Jake. We were both so young then."

Her grandmother chuckled. "I was even young back then."

But when Edna stopped and put a hand to her throat, Ella forgot everything else. "What is it, Granny?"

Edna pointed to an older young adult sitting near Jake. "Him," her grandmother said. "Percy Edmunds or Edson, I believe is his name. He was one of the summer interns who helped the youth director." Then she turned concerned eyes on Ella. "And honey, he helped paint a mural on the nursery wall. He was a college freshmen and about to go into his second year. Majoring in art."

Jake's phone buzzed at about the same time he noticed something significant back at the park where this nightmare had begun. "It's Ella," he told the sheriff, his gaze watching the woman running on the old jogging path.

He hastily pointed to the woman. "We interviewed her the first day Ella and I came out here."

The sheriff nodded and hurried after the woman.

"Hello?" Jake said into the phone on the final ring before it went to message.

"Oh, good, I got you." She sounded out of breath.

"Yeah, everything okay?"

"I found someone, Jake. In the church directory. Granny remembered him."

"Name?" Jake asked, his muscles tensing, a rush moving over him like a hot wind.

"Percy Edson. He interned at the church and we have pictures of him sitting in the sanctuary the day I sang that solo of 'Precious Memories.'"

She paused and let out a breath. "He was just past his freshman year of college but he interned that summer for our youth department. He painted a mural in the nursery. I thought I'd go by there and compare—"

"Not without me," Jake said, running to find the sheriff.

He saw Sheriff Steward talking to the woman on the path. What was her name? Maria Parsons? "I'll be there to pick you up but right now we're talking to that woman again. Same one you and I questioned when we came out last week." He glanced toward the sheriff and the jogger. "Ella, don't leave without me."

"Okay. I've still got to compare the volunteer list so I'll do that while I wait."

"Good idea." He ended the call and headed toward the sheriff. The woman went on down the path before Jake reached them. He wished he could have questioned her again.

Jake quickly told the sheriff what Ella had said on the phone. "We need to get back and we need to run a background check on this guy."

Sheriff Steward got in his marked SUV and cranked it up. Jake was already fastening his seat belt.

"This might be our man," the sheriff said. Then he glanced back off into the woods. "That woman says she jogs here almost every day. Says a lot of people frequent this path but she hasn't seen anyone recently who matched our description."

Jake's mind wasn't on the Parsons woman right now. "Ella and I questioned her the first day we came back here. She claimed a hooded man ran right by her and she was right. We found one of the clues on the path but she only gave the same vague description. Nothing else even after I called her back to follow up. Mrs. Parsons?"

"That's the name she gave me," the sheriff replied. "Sweet lady. She had her pepper spray but I told her to be careful."

"She shouldn't be out here alone," Jake replied, still occupied with getting to Ella. "Odd that she's popped up twice now when we've been here investigating."

The sheriff shook his head. "Probably a nosey looky-look trying to find out what we know. She could easily hear any cars stopping here since, according to the address she gave, she lives just past the curve in the woods."

"I guess so," Jake said. "I'm calling in the name Ella gave us. The sooner we find out more about this Percy Edson, the sooner we might find Macey."

After he'd given the name to one of the detectives helping out, he turned back to the sheriff. "Mrs. Parsons saw a man in a black sweatsuit wearing the hood over his face the day Ella and I came back here to do a search. She was a little skinned up and flustered."

"Didn't mention it today," the sheriff said. "Maybe she forgot the details."

"That doesn't make sense," Jake replied. "We gave her a ride home and she asked Ella about what had happened five years ago."

"We can check her out again," Sheriff Steward suggested.

Jake nodded. "I'd like to question her again. She and

Luke are the only ones who've seen anyone matching our description other than Macey's friend Rachel." He jotted that in his pocket notebook. "But right now, I'd like to see what we can find out about this Percy Edson."

Ella glanced at her granny's almost-finished scarf, her mind searching for any outlets. Granny's latest attempt made her think of the red scarf they'd found. And Jake had mentioned seeing Maria Parsons again. What was it about those two things that she needed to connect? Ella closed her eyes and envisioned Maria Parsons. Trim, fashionable jogging attire and…a scarf. A red knit scarf. It didn't mean anything, but it could mean everything.

"Granny, does anyone from church attend your knitting meetings?"

Edna's fingers stilled on her deft needles. "Sure, lots of people. We meet at church sometimes or other times in people's houses."

Ella's gut was still burning from finding out about Percy Edson, so she went with her instincts. "Do you know a Mrs. Parsons?"

"You mean Maria?" Granny asked, her eyes widening.

Ella's stomach lurched, the coffee she'd drunk boiling over into hot acid. "Yes, Maria. She lives over…near the old park."

Granny dropped her knitting. "You mean the park near where…where Jake found you that night?"

Ella nodded. "Yes, ma'am. She jogs on the old path. Jake and I talked to her the first day we went out together. She saw a man jogging. He pushed her off the path and ran away."

Her grandmother glanced to where Grandpa and Zip both lay sleeping, one in the recliner and the other by his feet. "I only know her from our knitting group. She rarely attends services. Is she okay?"

"She's fine," Ella said, careful not to overreact. "But Jake mentioned they'd seen her again today. On the same path."

Granny pushed at her glasses. "Maria's a quiet woman. Keeps to herself but she is big on fitness. Loves knitting. Says she stays in the house a lot so it gives her something to do. She comes to the meetings every now and then, but she's never hosted one."

Ella thought about how healthy Maria Parsons looked. She obviously got out and got her exercise each day. She was pretty tall for a woman, too. "Why does she stay inside so much?"

Granny frowned. "She mentioned a grown son who was in an accident a few years ago and he's now in a wheelchair."

The breath Ella had been holding released, causing her to feel faint. Her mind was playing tricks on her to the point of suspecting little old ladies of doing dire things. "Oh, that's horrible. No wonder she takes those daily jogs."

"Yes, probably one of the few times she gets to be alone with her thoughts."

Ella thought about the day they'd met Mrs. Parsons. "But she's a widow, right?"

"Yes, her second marriage, I believe. They'd only been married a little while before he died of a heart attack. Lived in Dallas but she had property here so she moved back. I declare, I don't think I've ever heard her mention his name."

Ella grabbed the volunteer sign-in list and searched for yesterday's date. When she'd found that, she searched the names and sign-in times. And found M. Parsons. She'd signed in yesterday morning and she'd worked one of the phones down in the kitchen command center. Granny might not have seen her at all.

Ella's phone buzzed. "That's Jake. We're going to the

church to check out the mural and then maybe back to question Mrs. Parsons again." Her instincts on high, Ella whistled. "I think I'll take Zip with us."

Ella's grandmother gave her a worried glance. "Everything okay? I mean, Jake will be with you, right?"

"Yes, of course." When Zip got up to follow her, Ella patted his head. "Let's go, boy." If anything happened to her, Zip would find his way home to warn someone.

Grabbing her coat, she hurried out to hop into Jake's truck. He had it cranked and ready. He eyed Zip but didn't protest.

"Sheriff Steward is running a check on Percy Edson right now. I told him to do one on the Parsons woman, too. Something about that woman—"

"Bothers you?" Ella asked, nodding. "I found out she's in my grandmother's knitting club—and she manned one of the phones yesterday. That red scarf... Jake, it's made of some of the same knitting yarns my grandmother uses. A new kind of weave. I remember Mrs. Parsons had on a similar scarf the first time we saw her." She hesitated then added. "And Granny said she has a grown son who was in a bad accident a few years ago. He's in a wheelchair now."

Jake's frown deepened. "I do find it mighty convenient that she's showed up twice now when we've been over there investigating. You think she took that message you found?"

"She had to have, but why wouldn't she have told anyone about it?" Ella couldn't stop her mind from putting two and two together. "Maybe no one called at all. Maybe she was sent here to leave that message."

Jake sped up, his gaze hitting on Ella. "She could be involved. Maybe those slippers belonged to her." He shook his head. "She could have easily left that message I found on the path in the woods. Could have been waiting and watching."

"Or she's just curious and she's watching the woods," Ella suggested, hoping it was the truth. "And she might not have thought anything about the phone message yesterday."

"But my gut is telling me to check her out," Jake replied, his tone grim. "All this time, she might be withholding information—or worse."

"Or she could be scared," Ella said, trying to rule out every scenario. "She was pretty shook up that day we found her."

"She knew who you were, Ella."

"She recognized me from the news stories."

"How?" He whirled the truck into the empty churchyard. "If she moved here right after we rescued you, how did she immediately recognize you? You've changed your hair."

"And why would anyone move into that house near that old fishing camp?" Ella asked, her breath growing more and more shallow and shaky. "Jake, you don't think—"

He grabbed her cold hand. "We're gonna find out, one way or another."

TWENTY-ONE

The church glistened white and pristine in the early afternoon sunshine. Ella glanced at the office and saw the closed sign on the door.

"Our minister and the secretary usually shut down the office and take an hour for lunch," she explained to Jake. "Maybe the custodian left the children's wing open since people come and go all day."

A van was parked near the door to the classroom and fellowship hall. "That's the custodian's van," she told Jake. "Let's see if we can find him."

"What's his name?" Jake's impatience shouted inside his voice.

"Bill Stratmore. He's been working here for years," Ella said, glancing at the van. "I think that's his vehicle."

"We'd better make sure," Jake retorted. He keyed the license plate number into his phone. "I'll see if I can find him."

Ella got out and let Zip out. "Stay," she ordered. The big dog whimpered in protest but he lay down on the concrete walkway toward the education building.

They hurried behind the church proper and pushed at the glass door to the education building. It was unlocked so Ella headed to the nursery.

"We'll take a look and get out of here," she suggested. "I'd like to go with you to question Mrs. Parsons again."

"I thought you were through with me," Jake said on a low whisper.

His words stung at Ella. She didn't want to be through with him, but they had a lot to get around before she could tell him that. "Not now," she retorted. "I need to know, Jake. Starting with this mural."

His tone went soft. "You and me both." He headed down the short hallway.

Ella reached the door marked Nursery. It was standing open and empty, so Ella entered and stopped to study the colorful mural covering one entire wall. She stood there for several minutes, taking it in.

Jake came in right behind her and let out a hiss of breath. "I didn't find the custodian."

"Amazing," Ella said, her gaze moving over the tall pines, bright green cypress trees and colorful swamp azaleas and redbud trees dotting the beautiful landscape.

An animated alligator lay across an old log, his grinning brown snout full of bright white teeth. Several turtles lined a grouping of rocks and stumps, their heads lifted as if in conversation. Deep blue water cascaded down a small white-tipped waterfall and settled into a dark pool. Nearby, a rustic houseboat floated away from the shore, the welcoming deck holding two rocking chairs. The mural was inviting and cartoonish—perfect for a room that would normally be filled with toddlers and preschoolers.

But the signature hidden among the palmetto palms and cypress knees caught Ella's attention. *Sacred Scenes.*

Outside, Zip let out a couple of barks. When Ella heard the dog's agitated growls, she knew someone was approaching. Then Zip went quiet. Ella listened and finally turned to where Jake stood near the door, his gun drawn. And then her world turned into a nightmare. A person wearing a baseball cap and dark shades came around the doorway and slammed something hard against Jake's head. He went down with a groan and a thump and lay there, unmoving, and bleeding from his head. His phone went flying and landed underneath a tiny wooden table.

The person held a gun on Ella and lifted Jake's gun off the floor and shoved it in a pocket. "I gave Zip some treats to calm him down. Your dog and I have become good buddies over the last few days."

Ella kept her eyes on Jake until the person spoke. Then she whipped her gaze around and saw what should have been evident from the beginning.

"Mrs. Parsons." Wearing a dark knit scarf around her throat.

"I see you figured things out," the disguised woman said, her smile as serene as the scene behind Ella. "You tried to kill my son and left him for dead—crippled him so he'll never walk again. It's finally time for you to reap what you've sown." She motioned with the gun. "C'mon on now. Come with me."

Ella realized too late that she hadn't brought her weapon. She glanced at Jake but he lay so still and quiet across the bright area rug she wondered if he'd ever wake up.

"Jake?" she called as she hurried toward him.

The woman pushed at Ella's chest. "Stop right there."

Ella's heart seemed to shrink but its beat increased in an urgent pounding that warned her of things to come. She wanted to call out to Jake again, but she was so stunned she couldn't move.

"Where are you taking me?" Ella asked, trying to go for her phone.

"Hands up," Mrs. Parsons retorted, the gun in Ella's face. "And hurry now. We don't have much time. Oh, and I'll take that cell phone."

Ella reluctantly gave the woman her phone. If Jake woke

up, he'd have to know where she was being taken. She slid a quick glance at his phone underneath the table, then prayed he'd call for backup.

She hoped and prayed he'd wake up. *Just open your eyes. Jake, please don't be dead. Please.*

But when Maria Parsons pulled her past Jake's still body, Ella took one last look back, her gaze moving from Jake to the beautiful flower-encrusted cross sitting on a nearby shelf.

That cross was the last thing she saw before Maria Parsons put a dark cloth bag over her face and told her to get in the van and duck down. She could hear Zip growling and barking, but somehow the woman managed to distract him—probably with another dog treat. They were in the van before Zip could reach her. Mrs. Parsons was a swift runner, after all.

Jake came out of a black fog, a hand on his arm tugging at him. "Hey, wake up. Jake, are you all right?"

He moaned as a throbbing pain splintered through his head with a thundering force. "I'm alive," he managed. Then reality came flooding back. "Ella?" He tried to sit up, but his head protested and a wave of dizziness overcame him. Trying again, he said, "I have to get to Ella."

"Hold on, son," Wilson Terrell said, his gray eyes washed with fear. "I was hoping you'd know where she got off to."

"Help me up," Jake said, his mind coming back to life, his nerves jingling like old chains. "She took Ella. That woman—"

Wilson got him to a chair then Jake glanced up to find the entire room crawling with law enforcement people. "Where is Ella?" he asked, his hand gripping Wilson's shirtsleeve.

"We don't know," Sheriff Steward said from behind Wilson. "Jake, Edna told us Ella found Maria Parsons's name on the volunteer list and suspected she might be involved in this case. When y'all didn't answer your phones or return home, she got worried and reported to us." He glanced out the door. "Then Zip showed up without y'all...."

Jake groaned. "It was her. She came in here and hit me over the head and she must have taken Ella." He glanced around and saw his phone under the table. "The man who painted this mural also painted the one on the barn. She must know him somehow." He remembered what Ella had told him. "She has a crippled son in a wheelchair."

He pointed to his phone. "I called in the plates on the van we saw outside. Maybe we got a hit."

The sheriff rushed to get Jake's phone, his gloved hands clutching it with a firm grip. "I'll make sure we find out."

Wilson turned back to Jake. "The custodian came back from lunch and found you passed out and called 911. We got paramedics on the way."

Jake shook his head. "I'll be okay. I gotta find Ella."

He tried to stand again, but when he saw bright, heated stars, he sank back down. Frustration colored his next words. "Her house...need to check the Parsons house."

"We're on it," the sheriff responded. "That plate you called in—stolen. We've put out an APB and a BOLO. You get yourself checked, Jake. We'll keep you informed."

Jake finally stood. "No, I'm going with you."

Ella shivered with cold, her body recoiling from what might happen next. She lay in the back of the big van, her mind whirling with images she'd tried so hard to forget. Trying desperately to grasp the situation and how they'd missed this angle from the very beginning, she struggled with her bound hands and feet and struck on something metal. Careful not to alert Maria Parsons, Ella moved her sneakered foot over the object in the back of the big van. Some sort of machine with wheels?

A big open van and a machine with wheels.

A wheelchair? The woman had told Ella her son was crippled.

"Be still back there," Maria shouted, her voice rasping with rage. "I should have killed you myself but I promised I'd wait."

Ella swallowed back bile and tried to think. "Are you taking me to him?"

"What do you think?" Maria asked, her tone smug now. "Of course he's waiting for you. That's been his plan all along. He gives the orders and I follow through. Always been that way with us. He's my big baby."

Ella made mental notes as the vehicle bumped over roads and made turns. They'd turned left out of the church. The opposite direction of Maria's house on the other side of the lake. Which meant no one would know where she was or how to find her. They'd check the house first.

"Is he your son?" she asked, hope warring with apprehension inside her mind. Had the killer planned this ambush for five years? Ella prayed she'd find Macey alive. "Where is the girl?"

"Shut up." The van stopped and a door opened. But before Ella could move, the driver's-side door slammed shut again. "They won't find you. I disguise this van all the time with different signs on the doors. Works every time."

No one would think much about stopping a service or delivery van with a business sign on each side.

Ella gave up and lay still and listened for what seemed like an eternity. Did she hear a train whistle? A touring train went around part of the lake but they couldn't be that close to a train station. Unless they were close to a town. When the van slowed, Ella strained to hear.

And she immediately heard the sounds of cars swishing by and…a crowd, people talking and laughing, the echoes of their ordinary gestures piercing her with such a yearning, she wanted to cry. Then she heard a choir singing Christmas songs.

Where was this madwoman taking her?

And then Ella knew. They were right smack dab in the middle of the Christmas Festival. Today was the opening ceremony in the huge state park located on the lower end of the lake.

Jake pushed at the paramedic's hand. "I said I'm okay. Just bandage me and let me sign a release."

The young man gave him a heavy frown and shook his head. "I've heard you're kind of hard to deal with, Ranger Cavanaugh."

"Then you heard right," Jake retorted. "Now let me up before I show you exactly how hard I am to deal with."

With a grunt, the young man dug into his supplies and found a square piece of gauze and some tape. "You need to be checked. You probably have a concussion."

"I only see one of you," Jake said, waiting impatiently while the medic doctored him and handed him the release. "Thank you," he said, hastily scrawling his signature. Then he got out of the bus before the man changed his mind and tied Jake down.

Still wobbly, Jake faked his way toward where the sheriff had placed a huge map on the back of a patrol car. "The Parsons house is located here, to the south of the church," the sheriff continued after shooting a surprised glare at Jake. "But the custodian said he saw a white van similar to his own turning to the left out of the churchyard."

Jake blinked away his double vision and inhaled. "Karnack's in that direction. Big festival there. Surely the woman wouldn't dare go into a crowd."

"We've got people over that way searching for the van

right now, but we got lots of vans around here," the sheriff said. "The festival's in the big state park and we all know they'll be plenty of vans of all colors parked there, for that matter. What better place to take a hostage and get lost in the crowd?" He rubbed his whiskers. "She probably changed the plates again, too."

Jake's pulse quickened and adrenaline rushed through his veins. "Let's get going."

"You will not drive," the sheriff warned. He pointed to a deputy. "Let Deputy Richards take you."

Jake didn't argue. He just prayed Deputy Richards knew how to go over the speed limit. "Get us there fast, son," Jake said on a growling command. The young deputy turned on the siren lights and hit the gas.

A few minutes later, the patrol car pulled into the mass of traffic crawling into the park. "I'll get us past all of this, sir," Richards said. He kept on the siren and waited to make sure no one was in his path, then turned down a lane into the shady parking area.

"Let me out here," Jake said, unleashed energy tearing through him. His head was still pounding, but his heart had already burst to pieces. His daughter and now Ella—again.

He'd failed in the worst kind of way.

Praying that he wasn't too late, Jake stalked through the crowd, searching for anything and anyone who might be connected to Maria Parsons and the Dead Drop Killer. He intended to end this thing before the sun went down.

Ella felt the rush of cold air when Maria Parsons opened the wide van door and leaned in. "I'm gonna take this cover off your head, but you need to understand I still have the gun and I will use it. I don't care who gets caught in the cross fire, either," Maria said, her voice sugary sweet and Southern. "Got it?"

Ella nodded, her mind spinning with the hope that

maybe someone would recognize her. She wasn't going to try to get away. She wanted to find Macey. But she could leave a trail. She reached up to push hair off her face and managed to free one of her tiny dangling earrings.

"You make a move and not only will I shoot into this crowd, but you'll die never knowing if that Macey girl is alive or dead." Maria poked the gun against Ella's chest. "I can take a few more with me, too."

"I said I understand," Ella retorted in a firm tone, the earring in her hand. "Now get on with it."

Maria laughed. "Anxious to be reunited with…my Percy? You weren't very nice to him all those years ago. Barely even noticed him, then went out and became an FBI agent. He sure didn't like that. Had to find other girls to… satisfy his crush on you. Maybe now you'll reconsider."

Ella didn't dare make a retort to that question. She just gritted her teeth and kept praying. Had she brought this on herself in some unknowing way?

"Now slide over here and step out of the van," Maria said. She had on dark shades and a floppy pink hat and… dark pink moccasins. "Nobody's around right now and besides, they'll think I'm delivering flowers." She handed Ella a dark hat. "Put this on."

Ella did as she said, her eyes adjusting to the bright afternoon sunshine. In a few hours the sun would go down behind the tree line and it would get cold and dark. She shuddered, memories hitting her like a chilling rain. Looking around, she saw hundreds of people having a good time, all oblivious to her fears and anxieties. She dropped the gold earring near the door of the van.

"Look straight ahead," Maria cautioned. "Keep your hand on my elbow."

Ella obliged the woman, walking slowly and purposely, trying to leave her boot imprints in the soft earth. "Where are you taking me?"

"You'll see soon enough."

"Have you always lived on the lake?"

"Shut up," Maria warned with a smile.

They walked on toward the public boat dock, moving through the crowd with a slow, steady gait. Ella focused her gaze on the path but tried to make eye contact with anyone who got too close, praying someone would see her terror. If she tried to take Maria down, someone could get shot. And Maria was right about one thing. Even if Ella managed to call for help or tried to subdue the woman, she might never know where they were holding Macey. So she had to keep going with the woman.

They'd reached the shoreline when Maria poked her in the ribs. "We're getting on that houseboat." She nudged Ella toward the dock. "This will be the last time you see any of these people."

Ella dared to glance back toward the shore. She spotted a tall man wearing a light-colored cowboy hat standing off in the falling shadows. Jake. He'd found her. Or nearly. He was looking in the other direction.

TWENTY-TWO

Jake kept his shades on and searched for a white van. But with so many cars, trucks and delivery vans here, that search became futile. He did a full 360-degree scan of his surroundings, his gaze finally settling on a florist delivery van parked underneath a huge live oak. He hurried that way and rushed to the van. No windows in the back, just like the one they'd seen at the church. Searching around the van, he looked for anything that might help.

And then he saw it there on the ground, sparkling in the bright sunshine. Ella's earring. And shoe imprints pressed against the soft earth. Imprints just like the ones Ella's chunky boots always left. She was leaving him a trail.

He followed the footprints until they blended in with too many others. Then he glanced up at the shoreline of Caddo Lake.

The lake was full of all types of boats from canoes and rafts to speedboats and pontoons. Jake studied each one and moved on, trying to spot Ella. Then he saw a big white houseboat anchored at the nearby public landing. And two women wearing hats were about to board it. Ella and Mrs. Parsons.

Jake radioed Deputy Richards and gave him the boat's description and location. "I'm in pursuit."

"Sir, you need to wait for backup."

"Call it in, Deputy. I'm *in pursuit!*"

He didn't wait for approval. Pushing through the crowd, he kept his eyes on the boat, but double vision had him blinking and trying to refocus. If he could just make it on before they left the dock—

He was halfway there when a big pickup truck barreled onto the path and blocked his way and his vision. Skirting around it and right into a group of teenagers who refused to part, Jake finally found an opening. Regaining his equilibrium, he blinked again and searched the shoreline, his boots hitting the ground at a run now as he headed down to the water's edge. His head screaming in pain, his heart rocking against his chest like crashing waves, Jake scanned the sunlight glistening off the lake.

The houseboat had already pulled away from the landing and was now headed out into the channel.

Jake didn't stop to think. He decided to follow the shoreline on foot and catch up with the big boat. He'd swim out to it if he had to. But the faster he ran, the more winded and dizzy he became. When the houseboat rounded the curve in the water that would take it out away from the shoreline, Jake tried to leap across a fallen cypress limb. He tripped and landed, a wave of dizziness descending on him at the same time his boots hit the muddy ground. He skidded into the mud and felt a solid blackness once again falling toward him.

No. No. He grunted, his teeth clenching against the pain. But hard as he tried, Jake couldn't stop the murky, star-washed slashes of white-hot agony stabbing against his head. With one last grunt, he tried to lift himself up out of the mud but his body felt weighted, chains of pain dragging him back down.

The image of Ella with that woman stayed front and center in his mind and then he blacked out.

* * *

Ella watched through dirty windows as the sun went down behind the tall pines and the dense cypress trees, her mind centered on staying alive to see the dawn of a new day. They'd taken her off the boat and now had her in a run-down building about a hundred yards off the water.

A cabin that seemed only too familiar. She'd been here before. Somehow, the search team had missed finding anyone there, but this was the same place she'd been held five years earlier.

Maria Parsons had tied her up and left her here alone, but Ella was doing her best to get out of the burning ropes. And while she worked with them, she called out and made note of her surroundings.

"Macey?"

No answer.

Ella gritted her teeth and tugged at the restraints, sweat popping out on her brow and dripping down her backbone in spite of the chill in the dank-smelling cabin. With no light to guide her, she struggled against the ropes and tried to ignore the sound of something scared and skittish tapping across the floor at a swift run.

"Macey, if you can hear me, it's okay. My name is Ella and I'm a friend of your father's. I'm going to get us out of this. Macey, please talk to me."

Ella hated the catch in her voice. But she wouldn't stop trying. "Macey, just call out if you can hear me and you're okay. My name is Ella."

Silence.

Ella's instincts shouted that they had Macey in this cabin. It was his cabin. The one where he'd brought her and held her those last few awful days. Had he murdered all the other girls here? Had he already killed Macey?

Ella worked at her wrists, twisting and pulling and tugging until she could feel the raw shreds of her skin peeling away like delicate tissue paper. The darkness swelled around her, cutting off her breath and reminding her of how alone she'd once felt here in this very place.

But you survived. You made it out.

Yes, she'd survived. She'd waited for him to return and then, hurting and frightened she'd convinced him to untie her so she could eat. She was so hungry, so cold, so dead inside. What did she have to lose?

He'd agreed because he knew, too, that she'd never make it out alive. Or so he'd thought. But he didn't know Ella, didn't know the kind of woman she'd become. So she'd waited until just the right moment to hit him across the head with the old two-by-four and then she'd grabbed his gun and shot at him. He'd cried out, so she'd run away, into the swamp, into the deep darkness that had once suffocated her. She took cover from him, but she could remember hearing him crawling toward her, crawling and calling her name. If she'd been stronger, she would have either killed him on the spot or taken him in. But she'd just stayed hidden in the dark.

Not this time. This time, she took in deep, calming breaths and thought about Jake and Macey. And she prayed.

"Ella?"

Ella blinked and stopped twisting. Had she just imagined that faint sound?

"Ella, I'm...I'm down here."

Macey!

"Where?" Ella struggled with the ties. She had to hurry. That woman would be back soon...with him. "I'm coming, Macey. I'll get us out of this. Just hang on, okay?"

"Okay. I'm scared."

"I know honey. I'm scared, too. But...I'll find you."

When Ella heard the sound of tires hitting on gravel and dirt, she twisted one last time and broke free, her wrists bleeding now.

* * *

Jake's eyes came open to total darkness. He was cold and wet…and mad. Grasping for his cell, he could barely see the missed calls. Hitting the first number, he moaned into the phone. "Jake Cavanaugh, Texas Ranger. I need help."

A few minutes later, Jake lay on an ambulance gurney on the way to the hospital. And he was fighting at his oxygen mask and calling the first responders names. He'd lost Ella. He'd lost Macey. He was lost in an angry delirium that threatened to take him under if he didn't get a grip on things.

So finally, he let them cart him into the emergency room and he waited until they'd checked him over and then after they thought they had him tucked in and drugged up for the night, he ripped everything that beeped and dripped off his body and slowly managed to get his muddy, dirty clothes back on and then he snuck out the back of the building. He called the one person who'd listen to him.

Ella's grandpa.

Wilson pulled up in a record fifteen minutes. "Get in," he said on an urgent command. "Before we get arrested."

Jake did as he was told and took comfort in the two shotguns snuggled against the gun rack on the back window of the old truck. "Did you bring extra ammo?"

"What do you think?" Wilson retorted.

"I think I know where they took her," Jake replied, deciding now was not the time to get into things with Ella's grandfather. Wilson had made no bones about Jake dragging Ella back into this mess, but they both loved her so they'd get things settled once Ella and Macey were safe.

He took a breath and prayed to that end. *Please Lord, let them stay alive. Help me to find them so I can hold them both close and tell them how much I love them.*

He finished his prayers and got back to action. "So I'm

guessing Maria Parsons has volunteered a lot over the last few days."

"Yep."

"And she must have been at your place today so she knew when we left."

"Yep. She was in a different car. According to everyone who's heard the news, she was the nicest little lady. Kept to herself but helped out when she could. A lot of people are in shock right now."

"I hear that," Jake replied. "We had her that first day. Right there. I'm thinking there never was a man on the path. She set us up."

"I think you're right. We got a call from Luke's parents. He woke up a few minutes ago and told them that the person in his room might have been a woman."

"That's what Luke must have been trying to tell us," Jake replied, glad for God's own timing. "But her son must have survived so she's seeking revenge."

"Maybe we'll get to ask them about that," Wilson said on a calm note. "Right before we—"

"Careful," Jake said, his mind boiling with that image. "I don't want you going to jail."

"Whatever it takes," Wilson replied. "I want him and anyone connected to him out of our lives. For good."

"We can agree on that," Jake replied. Then he told Wilson how to get to the woods where they'd found Ella five years ago. "I don't think the two officers who searched out there did a very thorough job. But we'll tear any buildings apart if we have to."

Wilson grunted. "Board by board."

Ella rushed toward the sound of Macey's cries. "Shh, honey, I'm right here." She saw the outline of a trapdoor in a corner of the only other room in the tiny cabin. An old iron-framed bed was halfway across the door, probably to keep it hidden and to make sure Macey couldn't push her way out. With a grunt, Ella shoved the bed away and tried to lift the door.

Footsteps hit the porch, followed by the sound of something whirring. The wheelchair?

Then she heard her name and she knew.

"Ella? Sweet Ella? Where are you hiding this time?"

Him. The Dead Drop Killer.

"She's here. I tied her up good and proper."

"Shut up, Mama."

"Don't tell me to shut up. I've killed for you and now I'm about to help you end this once and for all."

Ella twisted toward the trapdoor, trying with all her might to get it open so she could drop down inside with Macey. She heard Macey whimpering. The girl obviously knew who was coming.

And maybe what was to come, too.

Ella grunted and tugged at the heavy door, her arms stinging from the salty pain of sweat hitting her raw, jagged wounds. Her muscles tightened and tore but she kept pulling and tugging until she had the door open. She pushed one more time and it lurched against the wall with a loud shattering.

Ella fell away and gulped in air, her upper body numb with pain. Then she stared down into the black pit, the horror of her own nightmares staring her in the face. "Hold on, Macey," she said on a low whisper. "I'm coming."

The motor purred closer and then the door to the room swung open and a light shined into Ella's eyes, blinding her.

"Going somewhere, sweet Ella?"

Ella didn't stop to think. "Yes," she said. Then she lifted her legs over the opening and dropped down until her feet hit something solid.

Jake tried to get his bearings before he alerted the sheriff and the task force. They were off the beaten path, on an old dirt lane caked with mud and ruts. And they'd reached a crossroad.

"Which way?" Wilson asked, giving Jake a sideways glance.

"Let me think," Jake said. "I was on this road when I heard Ella. She'd seen the flashlight beam and she called out." He stopped, memories circling him like a clinging mist. "To the right." He hoped.

Wilson floored it, brittle mud kicking up with a crushing clarity as the vehicle bounced with a teeth-jarring swiftness up the old road. When they came around a curve, Jake held up his hand. "Cut the lights and turn off the engine. I'll go on foot from here."

"Make that *we*," Wilson said, reaching for the guns.

"You need to wait in the truck," Jake retorted.

"I'm going with you," Wilson said, his jaw set.

Jake didn't argue with him. "Stay behind me and cover me. We'll need to call for reinforcements."

Wilson shifted his chin in a nod, then got out of the truck.

Jake put a finger to his lips then motioned for Wilson to follow him. Fifteen minutes later, he could see the shadow of the building huddled in the moonlight. It sat squat and square on six-foot pilings, an old storage room underneath the main floor helping to hold the place up. The white van was parked beside the lean-to porch. He noticed a ramp had been added since last time he'd been here. He stopped, Wilson a few feet away, and listened to the night sounds. The woods and trees were eerily still, a biting cold settling against the night with a clinging wetness that cut to the bone.

Jake listened and then he heard it. A whirling sound. He stepped closer, careful not to make too much noise. The sound got louder. Closing his eyes, he didn't want to think what that sound might be. He turned back to check on Wilson and the older man pointed to the van.

Jake glanced that way and saw what Wilson had noticed. A wheelchair ramp on the open side of the van. Jake nodded, then looked at the ramp leading up to the two-story porch. Someone was in a wheelchair.

The killer?

Everything started falling into place then.

The Dead Drop Killer had survived. But he was obviously disabled now. So who'd killed the other girl and kidnapped Macey?

He had a sneaking suspicion he knew who that was.

But right now, he had to get into that cabin and save Ella and Macey. He prayed he wasn't too late. He hurried back to Wilson. "Call for backup and give them directions to stop up on the road and walk the rest of the way. No sirens."

Wilson nodded and pulled out his phone. "What are you gonna do?"

Jake tugged his hat down on his head. "I'm going in there and I'm not coming out until this is over."

TWENTY-THREE

"Now that was a stupid move."

Ella ignored the man talking to her from above and tried to get her bearings. She'd fallen a long way and her left ankle now throbbed and protested each time she put weight on it. "Macey?"

A whimper down below from the right corner.

Ella got on her hands and knees and felt around. Another trapdoor, but smaller…and open. "Are you okay?"

Another whimper. "Yesss."

Ella lifted herself over the opening and was about to jump again but she felt a rope ladder that went all the way up to the bigger door she'd found above. So this was how Maria Parsons got up and down. Ella went down the ladder to the hidden bottom, gritting her teeth against the pain in her right ankle. Hitting the hard floor, she stumbled around, groping for support until her eyes could adjust to the pitch darkness. She felt the cold stone wall and held to it, the shuddering of her body forcing her to keep moving.

She'd figured from the view of the trees through the moonlight out the dirty window above that the house had to be up on some sort of pilings. This room must have been built underneath the main cabin. Maybe as a storage area or garage. Or a prison with stone walls.

She moved around, but a bright light from above caused her to gasp and whirl, her gaze lifting.

"Ella, how can we talk if you're stuck down there and I'm stuck up here?"

"I don't want to talk to you," she retorted. "I came to take this girl home and that's what I plan to do."

"How?" Mrs. Parsons called out. "That room's sealed off. It's below the storage room, so those two goons y'all sent out didn't have a clue. We have a false floor. You won't make it out of here alive. We'll just shut you both in there and leave."

Ella decided to play along. "Go ahead. Your son can't hurt me now."

An angry grunt echoed down to her. "No, but I can. I've waited for this moment since the day he called me and told me he was hurt and left for dead—because of you. Barely survived but he held on until I could get here and get him help."

"I loved you, Ella," Percy shouted. "But you never even noticed me, didn't even want to talk to me. I had to find other girls to replace you but…Mama didn't like any of them, either."

"I still don't like her," Maria said on an angry wail. "Now let's get on with this."

"No, you promised me I'd get to see her again. Up close."

Ella didn't need the details right now. But she did need the truth. Moving closer to the shallow breathing she heard in the corner, she called out, "So you brought Percy home and nursed him back to health. Then you took over for him?"

"I found him down in that pit," Mrs. Parsons shouted. "Crawled back here and called me then he fell." A short sob followed. "Fell in that hole and almost died. I had a time getting him out, but we managed. We managed."

Silence. Giving Ella enough time to reach out and find a shivering figure huddled on a blanket in the corner. "Macey, I'm here."

The girl fell into her arms and held on for dear life. So did Ella. "It's okay. I'm here. We'll get out of this, I promise. You have to stay strong, okay?"

She felt the bobbing of Macey's head. Holding tight, she rocked the girl back and forth, tears piercing her eyes. Macey's soft sob mirrored those tears while Ella tried to process what Maria had told her. If they did get shut in here, Ella would never forgive herself. She'd die trying to get them out.

Ella heard whispering above. She strained to hear but soon the whispering turned into arguing.

"I told you this was a bad idea, bringing her back to this cabin. What if that Ranger remembers where he found her out there?"

"I don't care about the Ranger, Mama. I want you to help me get her back up here. I've waited for this and I'm gonna enjoy every minute of it."

"Percy, listen to me. I've done everything you asked. Now let's just close 'em up in there and leave before it's too late."

"No!" She heard the motor of the wheelchair whirl to a stop. "Quit being so jealous and get down there. Take the gun and make her come out."

Ella had to get Macey out of here before they took the ladder away and shut the big door. She held Macey close, his hand moving over the girl's hair. "Listen to me, honey. I might have to go back upstairs for a while."

Macey shook her head and sobbed.

"Just long enough to figure out how to get us out, okay?"

Stillness then a bobbing in agreement. "Don't leave me down here too long."

"I won't, I promise." Ella tugged away from the girl and stood on weak legs. "Hey, Percy?"

The arguing stopped and the light beamed down. "Ready to come up here and talk?"

"Yes," Ella replied. "I guess that would be wise on my part."

"Hold on."

More sharp words and footsteps scrambling.

With the beam of light coming down on them, Ella glanced back to where Macey sat against the wall, her gaze hitting on the girl's vacant, scared eyes.

"I'll be back soon," she whispered. "Macey, listen to me. Wait until after I'm up there and when you hear me calling your name, be ready to climb that rope and run out of this cabin. Can you do that?"

"I think so," Macey replied. "I've tried to…stay strong."

"You are strong," Ella replied. "Strong like your parents."

Strong like your daddy.

The flashlight shifted into Ella's eyes again. "You'd better not try anything," Maria Parsons called. "Or you'll both get left down there—just like my poor Percy."

"I want to talk to Percy," Ella said, already working her way up the ladder. When she reached the top, she glanced back down and heard Macey moving around.

Turning back she reached the last step and said one final prayer. Her only hope was to knock Maria Parsons out of the way and then figure out what to do after that.

Jake did a slow crawl up the wheelchair ramp toward the rickety porch of the cabin. This place was about as desolate and off the beaten path as you could get. No wonder it had been nearly impossible to find the first time. Holding his breath as he reached the porch, he kept his handgun close and listened. Two people were heavy into a discussion. Careful to only move in inch-size increments, Jake finally made it to the old window and slowly moved up against the wall, his breath held.

He glanced inside and saw Maria Parsons staring down an open spot in the floor while her son sat in a nearby motorized wheelchair.

Then Ella's head appeared. The storage room below? He almost jumped off the porch to check but decided he'd wait until Ella needed his help. She glanced back down one last time before she lifted herself out of the square opening.

Maria Parsons greeted her with a gun to her head.

Jake wanted to rush in and save her right now, but he held back so he could come up with a plan. The front door was to his left. Probably latched. He could shoot through the window but he might hit Ella. He watched and waited and prayed. And wondered if his daughter was down in that dark hole.

Ella stood and stared at Percy Edson. Shock at finally seeing his face clouded her system, but Ella didn't let that show. He'd gained weight and looked pudgy and bloated now, his once brown hair a dirty, gray-streaked mop.

Ella felt no fear, seeing what was left of the man who'd killed so many innocent young girls. Putting on her best front, she asked, "So you blame me for you being in that wheelchair?"

Percy backed the wheelchair away and stared at her for a long time. "I loved you, you know. And yet, I couldn't have you. You were too young the first time we met and too in love with *him.* So I had to wait for you to grow up. At least we had a few weeks together."

Ella swallowed the bile in her throat. "How'd that work out for you?"

Rage crested in his dark eyes. "Not so good, after all. But here we are, together again." He leaned up in the chair.

"I might not be able to do the…things I used to do. But I will enjoy watching you die even if I'll also regret it." He nodded toward the floor. "But I'll kill her first, of course."

"I don't think so," Ella said on a firm note.

He motioned to another chair. "My mama didn't tie you tight enough," he said. "If I could get up—"

"I'll make sure she's here to stay now," Maria Parsons said, her pistol pointed at Ella's head. She pushed Ella down into the chair and went around behind her. "I can't hold the gun and tie her, son. Wanna help out here?"

Percy shifted his chair toward Ella. "With pleasure."

Jake watched, his heart in his throat, and saw the determination cresting in Ella's eyes. She waited until Percy was behind the chair and then when his mother came around to the other side, Ella lifted up her leg and kicked Maria Parsons hard on the wrist, causing the pistol to fly out of the woman's hand and fall about a foot from the opening in the floor.

Jake didn't wait any longer. He turned and kicked the front door open and called out, "Texas Ranger. Put your hands up or I'll shoot."

After that, the roaring in his ears only parted when he heard Ella calling his daughter's name. Ella went down with Maria Parsons and wrestled the kicking, screaming woman onto her stomach and held her by sitting on her. When Jake touched a hand to her shoulder, she turned and gave him a surprised but grateful glance.

Percy cranked up the wheelchair and charged right toward Ella but Jake screamed at him to halt. Percy kept going, intent on running over both Ella and his mother. Ella grunted and rolled out of the way, pulling Mrs. Parsons with her. Jake shot at the wheelchair. Percy jerked but kept going.

Right toward the gaping open door down to the storage room.

"Macey?" Both Jake and Ella shouted. Jake started toward the opening.

And then, his daughter's head popped up out of the floor and before he could make a move, she grabbed the pistol lying on the floor and started shooting.

Percy's head flopped against his body and the chair kept going, one of its wheels hitting the heavy raised door to below before the chair flipped to its side, its wheels still grinding.

Macey jumped out of the way, her hands still holding the gun.

Her fingers still pulling the trigger.

Then, other than Maria Parsons's garbled sobs, the room went still and quiet. Jake rushed to Macey while Ella secured Mrs. Parsons.

"Macey, baby." He took his daughter into his arms and rocked her close, tears rolling down his face. "It's over, baby. It's all over."

Macey held tight to him but her eyes were on Ella.

Christmas Eve

Winter rustled through the leaves that danced against the yard, but inside the house Ella was safe and warm. She turned to smile at Granny.

Her grandmother smiled back. "Dinner's almost ready, honey. Wanna call the men in from the den?"

"Sure," Ella replied. "Maybe we can pull 'em away from that sports channel."

She walked under the archway and stopped, her heart filling with a tremendous joy. Zip lay curled up beside Macey on the big hooked rug in front of the fireplace. The teenager had taken an immediate liking to the dog when they'd first brought her home from the hospital. Macey had insisted on coming here first thing, to thank Ella.

Now Zip didn't want to leave Macey's side, either. Ella figured he sensed the girl's fears and he aimed to protect her. And since Macey and Jake had been spending a lot of time here, no one was gonna argue with that notion.

Ella felt the same. Macey was safe and in good shape physically, but her emotional wounds would take a long time to heal. Maria Parsons and her son, Percy, had dragged Macey all over East Texas, changing vehicles and keeping her hidden until they could get her back to the old deserted cabin and into the dark holding area. Ella knew some of what the girl was going through and she planned to be here to help Macey. With therapy and a close-knit circle around her, Macey should recover.

They'd finally found out the other girl's identity. Jennifer Gerald from Shreveport. A runaway who'd been in the wrong place at the wrong time. Maria Parsons had mistaken her for Macey a week before they'd taken Macey. At least her parents now knew what had happened to her. Jake and Ella had attended her memorial service.

After her second husband had died, Maria Parsons had taken over her son's crimes out of some sort of atonement and guilt. She'd tried to emulate him, but she'd gotten sloppy and scared. Her son's demands had driven her to do things she'd never wanted to do. Now she would probably be in prison for the rest of her life.

And yet, Ella couldn't feel sorry for the woman. She'd have to seek prayer and find peace about that.

Ella's gaze moved from the girl and the dog to the man sitting on the sofa, her heart filling up with love. Jake's eyes held hers and she smiled.

"Dinnertime," she announced, her gaze still on him. "We've got an entire Christmas feast waiting for y'all in there."

Grandpa pushed out of his recliner. "Smells so good, I thought you'd never come and get us. I've got my eye on a big juicy turkey leg and I kept thinking about it during the Christmas Eve service."

Edna shook her head. "Wilson Terrell, you should have been listening to the beautiful music."

"You can eat that turkey leg right after we say grace," Ella replied. "Along with all the trimmings."

Her grandpa glanced at Jake then back to her. "Macey, how about you and Zip help me get the tea glasses ready?" He winked at the girl. "And we might just grab us a home-made yeast roll while we're at it."

Macey jumped up, grinning. She'd kind of adopted Ella's grandparents as her own, too. She hurried past Ella, her pretty eyes holding a shy smile. "You two behave," she whispered.

Ella gave her a poke. "Same to you when Luke comes by later, okay?"

"Yes, ma'am," Macey said, still smiling.

Jake walked up to Ella. "What was that all about?"

"Girl talk," Ella replied, her hand reaching for his.

He took her hand and pulled her into his arms. "I could get used to this."

Ella wondered about that. "Really? I mean, can you get used to me? Ever?"

He lifted away to stare down at her, his eyes as bright as the lights on the tree. "I've always been used to you. I've just never understood you."

"Will you try?" she asked, her heart telling her to be brave and just go for what she wanted.

"For the rest of my life," he said on a soft note. "I owe you so much."

"I don't want gratitude and I don't want attitude," she retorted. "This time, I want it to be right."

He kissed her on the nose then looked into her eyes. "Do you want to be my wife? Finally?"

Ella wanted that more than anything. "Can you live

with me being a farmer now? Or with me being anything else, finally?"

"More than I could have lived with you being…not here."

"Jake, we can't fight about that kind of stuff anymore. I might decide I'd rather be a fighter pilot or something. I need to know you'll support that."

He gave her an adorable, confused stare. "Have you joined the Air Force or the Navy?"

"Neither," she said with a grin. "Not yet, at least."

He kissed her until she forgot everything but being in his arms. Then he said, "I can live with you because I love you and I can't live without you—no matter what you want to do for the rest of your life. How's that?"

The last of Ella's doubts faded away. "I love you, too. Can you live with me here? Or should I plan on moving to Tyler?"

He glanced around. "I've always loved this place. Macey seems to love it here, too."

"Well, we've got room to build our own house down near the big kitchen. If you're man enough to let me do that for us."

"Is that a yes?" he asked, grinning down at her.

"Is that a yes from you?" she retorted.

Jake pushed a hand through her hair and gave her a look that promised a lot of tomorrows. "I reckon it is," he said. "Marry me and I'll show you the kind of man I can be."

Ella laughed at that. "I can't wait to find out."

He gave her a lopsided smile. "You and me. Side by side."

She kissed him. "Glad we got that settled. Now let's eat."

"I thought y'all would never make up your minds," Grandpa called from the dining table. Zip barked his own reply.

Jake and Ella laughed and then, together, they walked into the dining room to have Christmas Eve dinner with their family. And to count their many blessings.

* * * * *

Dear Reader:

This was a tough story for me. I'm a scaredy-cat and I don't care for disturbing stories but when a story pops in my head, I try to run with it. In many ways, writing this book helped me to overcome any fears I might have when writing such a grisly story and reinforced to me that faith and love always win out, no matter the outcome.

Ella and Jake had a long history that kept bringing them back together. They not only had to trace a serial killer but they also had to reevaluate their feelings for each other and learn how to express those feelings in a way that would bring them peace and love, not tear them apart. They allowed God's grace to help both of them heal. That is the lesson I learned. We all have scars that need healing and his love can do that for us.

I hope this story kept you turning the pages. It sure kept me up for a lot of nights!

Until next time, may the angels watch over you. Always!

Lenora Worth

Questions for Discussion:

1. Jake and Ella were high school sweethearts. How do you think it feels to love someone while watching them walk away?

2. Jake had a problem with Ella being exposed to dangerous situations. Do you think his objections were valid? Or did his protest stem from a deeper fear?

3. Ella found peace in her life by turning back to her faith and to the land she loved. Have you ever changed careers in order to find more peace in your life?

4. Ella gave up her goal of being an FBI agent after she went through a horrible trauma. Do you think she made the right decision?

5. Jake was forced to reexamine his motives for letting Ella go the first time. After she told him the truth of why she left the FBI, he finally understood just how strong she'd become. Have you ever overcome something traumatic and come out triumphant with the help of your faith?

6. Ella loved her farm-to-table restaurant because it gave her something positive to do in her life. Have you ever let go of the past by taking a chance on a different way of life?

7. Jake loved his daughter but he didn't really know her. He started doubting her and imagining all sorts of things that might give him answers. Have you ever

had a loved one who might have kept secrets from you? How did you handle that?

8. Ella's grandparents played a large role in nurturing her after she'd been through so much pain. Do you have a strong family network to help support you in times of trouble?

9. We all try to trust people but have you ever had an instinctive feeling about someone you want to trust? Did your instincts prove you were correct?

10. Do you have a loved one who works in a dangerous situation? If so, how do you deal with your fears and concerns for that person?

11. East Texas is a great place with beautiful countryside. But even the most tranquil spots can hold dark secrets. Have you ever lived in a place that both intrigued you and frightened you? Did you rely on God for strength?

12. What did you think of this book? Did it keep you reading or did you want to tell the characters a thing or two? What would you have done in Ella's or Jake's shoes?

COMING NEXT MONTH FROM
Love Inspired® Suspense

Available December 2, 2014

HER CHRISTMAS GUARDIAN
Mission: Rescue • by Shirlee McCoy

Scout Cramer's young daughter is kidnapped while Scout is on the run from her troubled past. Can hostage rescue expert Boone Anderson risk his life—and his heart—to bring them together again?

THE YULETIDE RESCUE
Alaskan Search and Rescue • by Margaret Daley

A plane crash leaves Dr. Aubrey Mathison stranded in the Alaskan wilderness during the Christmas season. Search and Rescue leader David Stone arrives just in time, but together they'll discover there are more dangers lurking on the snowy horizon.

COLD CASE JUSTICE • by Sharon Dunn

Rochelle Miller thinks she's left her past behind as a witness to murder, until the criminal reappears. This time when she runs, she'll have handsome paramedic Matthew Stewart to keep her son safe...and the killer at bay.

NAVY SEAL NOEL
Men of Valor • by Liz Johnson

Abducted by a drug cartel, Jessalynn McCoy must rely on her former best friend—navy SEAL Will Gumble—to get her home in time for Christmas. But can she bring herself to trust the man who left her behind years ago?

SILVER LAKE SECRETS • by Alison Stone

After her life is put on the line, Nicole Braun refuses to allow her little boy to get caught up in the danger. Too bad the only one she can trust to protect her, police chief Brett Eggert, also has the power to break her heart.

TREACHEROUS INTENT • by Camy Tang

It's Liam O'Neill's job as a skip tracer to find private investigator Elisabeth Aday's missing client. When rival gangs come after them for information, they're thrown together in a race against the clock.

———————

REQUEST YOUR FREE BOOKS!
2 FREE RIVETING INSPIRATIONAL NOVELS
PLUS 2 FREE MYSTERY GIFTS

Love Inspired®
SUSPENSE

YES! Please send me 2 FREE Love Inspired® Suspense novels and my 2 FREE mystery gifts (gifts are worth about $10). After receiving them, if I don't wish to receive any more books, I can return the shipping statement marked "cancel." If I don't cancel, I will receive 4 brand-new novels every month and be billed just $4.74 per book in the U.S. or $5.24 per book in Canada. That's a savings of at least 21% off the cover price. It's quite a bargain! Shipping and handling is just 50¢ per book in the U.S. and 75¢ per book in Canada.* I understand that accepting the 2 free books and gifts places me under no obligation to buy anything. I can always return a shipment and cancel at any time. Even if I never buy another book, the two free books and gifts are mine to keep forever.

123/323 IDN F5AC

Name _____ (PLEASE PRINT)

Address _____ Apt. #

City _____ State/Prov. _____ Zip/Postal Code

Signature (if under 18, a parent or guardian must sign)

Mail to the Harlequin® Reader Service:
IN U.S.A.: P.O. Box 1867, Buffalo, NY 14240-1867
IN CANADA: P.O. Box 609, Fort Erie, Ontario L2A 5X3

**Are you a current subscriber to Love Inspired Suspense books
and want to receive the larger-print edition?
Call 1-800-873-8635 or visit www.ReaderService.com.**

* Terms and prices subject to change without notice. Prices do not include applicable taxes. Sales tax applicable in N.Y. Canadian residents will be charged applicable taxes. Offer not valid in Quebec. This offer is limited to one order per household. Not valid for current subscribers to Love Inspired Suspense books. All orders subject to credit approval. Credit or debit balances in a customer's account(s) may be offset by any other outstanding balance owed by or to the customer. Please allow 4 to 6 weeks for delivery. Offer available while quantities last.

Your Privacy—The Harlequin® Reader Service is committed to protecting your privacy. Our Privacy Policy is available online at www.ReaderService.com or upon request from the Harlequin Reader Service.
We make a portion of our mailing list available to reputable third parties that offer products we believe may interest you. If you prefer that we not exchange your name with third parties, or if you wish to clarify or modify your communication preferences, please visit us at www.ReaderService.com/consumerchoice or write to us at Harlequin Reader Service Preference Service, P.O. Box 9062, Buffalo, NY 14269. Include your complete name and address.

LIS13R

"Robin," Ethan said, just before his face appeared in the church belfry's open trapdoor, "come on up. It's perfectly safe."

He reached down a gloved hand as she put a foot on the bottom rung of the wrought-iron ladder.

"How does this thing work?"

"It's very simple. There's a tall pole with a hook on one end. I used it to slide open the trap and then pull down the ladder. When I'm done, I'll use it to push the ladder back up and lift it over the locking mechanism, then slide the trap closed."

"I see."

"Oh, you haven't seen anything yet," he told her, grasping her hand and all but lifting her up the last few rungs to stand next to him on a narrow metal platform. In their bulky coats, they had to stand pressed shoulder to shoulder. "Take a look at this." He swung his arm wide, encompassing the town, the valley beyond and the snow-capped mountains surrounding it all.

"Wow."

"Exactly," he said. "There's a part of Psalms 98 that says, 'Let the rivers clap their hands, let the mountains sing together for joy…' Seeing the view like this, you can almost feel it, can't you? The rivers and mountains praising their Creator."

"I never thought of rivers and mountains praising God," she admitted.

"Scripture speaks many times of nature praising God and testifying to His wonders."

"I can see why," she said reverently.

"So can I," he told her, smiling down at her with those warm brown eyes.

Her breath caught in her throat. But surely she was reading too much into that look. That wasn't appreciation she saw in his gaze. That was just her loneliness seeking connection. Wasn't it? Though she had never felt this sudden, electrical link before, as if something vital and masculine in him reached out and touched something fundamental and feminine in her. She had to be mistaken.

He was a man of God, after all.

Even if she couldn't help thinking of him as just a man.

Will Robin and Ethan find love for Christmas,
or will her secrets stand in their way?
Find out in HER MONTANA CHRISTMAS
by Arlene James, available December 2014 wherever
Love Inspired® books and ebooks are sold.

Love Inspired® SUSPENSE

RIVETING INSPIRATIONAL ROMANCE

THE YULETIDE RESCUE

by

MARGARET DALEY

MISTLETOE AND MURDER

When Dr. Bree Mathison's plane plummets into the Alaskan wilderness at Christmastime, she is torn between grief and panic. With the pilot—her dear friend—dead and wolves circling, she struggles to survive. Search and Rescue leader David Stone fights his way through the elements to save her. David suspects the plane crash might not have been an accident, spurring Bree's sense that she's being watched. But why is someone after her? Suddenly Bree finds herself caught in the middle of a whirlwind of secrets during the holiday season. With everyone she cares about most in peril, Bree and her promised protector must battle the Alaskan tundra and vengeful criminals to make it to the New Year.

ALASKAN

+ SEARCH RESCUE

Risking their lives to save the day

Available December 2014
wherever Love Inspired
books and ebooks are sold.

Find us on Facebook at
www.Facebook.com/LoveInspiredBooks

LIS44637